Nabilah Khan is a South African expat who has been living in the UAE for the past few years. She loves spending time with her husband and two young girls, and writing lighthearted, feel-good stories that make people smile.

For my husband Ahmad, this story wouldn't have seen the 'sunshine' had it not been for your undying support and belief in me.
For my girls, anything is possible.

Nabilah Khan

YOU ARE MY SUNSHINE

AUSTIN MACAULEY PUBLISHERS™

LONDON * CAMBRIDGE * NEW YORK * SHARJAH

ISBN – 9789948781974 – (Paperback)
ISBN – 9789948781981 – (E-Book)

Application Number: MC-10-01-2455192
Age Classification: 21+

Printer Name: iPrint Global Ltd
Printer Address: Witchford, England

First Published 2023
AUSTIN MACAULEY PUBLISHERS FZE
Sharjah Publishing City
P.O Box [519201]
Sharjah, UAE
www.austinmacauley.ae
+971 655 95 202

I've loved every process of creating this character and her story, and each step taken to get this book in your hands.

I'm so grateful to you, my reader, for taking a chance on this book, my debut novel. It's been such a pleasure having you on this journey with me and I hope it's been an enjoyable read for you!

To my husband: Words cannot express how much I cherish you. You always support every crazy idea I have. You are always ready to get your hands dirty in helping me achieve all my dreams and ambitions. I am because you are.

To my daughters: You girls are my stars, the sunshine in my sky, the light in my life. This is for you. It's never too late to try something new.

To my parents and siblings: Thank you for all the excitement that you bring to the table, and thank you for always being in my corner, no matter what.

To Caron Rademan: Your thoughtful recommendations have been invaluable in creating what this book is today.

To Rachel Hitchcock: My immense gratitude goes out to you for your dedication and diligence to ensure that even the smallest of details were consistent.

To my beta readers: For offering valuable insights and kind words that really motivated me to take my story to the best version of itself possible. I can't thank you enough for believing in my work!

To everyone at Austin Macauley: Thank you for working tirelessly to bring this book into my readers' hand.

Chapter 1

My left forefinger pecks at the keyboard. Letters ponderously form words… Every now and then, I glance at my story board. I rip off an old pink Post-it note and replace it with a fresh blue one. I sip my coffee, which is cold and bitter from being reheated too many times. I continue typing, eyes burning from staring at the bright screen.

The teens trudged through the dark forest. The wind whistled through the trees; shadows from the moonlight danced on the ground. Jamie checked her phone again. Google Maps kept rerouting and she only had ten percent of her battery left. Isabella's phone had died two hours ago…

I hit backspace on the entire line. There is no way anyone, let alone two teens in the 21st century would forget their battery pack. Hell, I treat my battery pack like one of my vital organs inconveniently situated outside my body.

I continue.

Isabella dug out her battery pack from her bag and shoved it into her phone. For the next few hours, they would be OK. She sighed in relief. Jamie, already a few steps ahead of her, hissed for her attention. "Come on Izzie," she whispered, her voice dry and strained. "I think I see something."

Their eyes rested on a wooden cabin, dim light flickering in the windows. Jamie lifted the bloody knife carefully from her bag. It was the one she had taken out of her best friend's abdomen earlier that evening. As they got closer, they slowed down, fighting to control their breathing. They inched forward, careful not to make any sound that would attract whoever was inside. Jamie looked at Isabella, who nodded, and she pushed the door open.

I yawn and lean back in my chair, closing my laptop. My eyelids weigh heavily as I try to keep them open. No luck. Rosie will have to wait for this chapter.

Rosana Patel is one of my closest friends— and book editor. She is the one who convinced me that I should try my hand at writing a horror novel after we'd graduated. I've always thought that it might be a bad idea to mix your personal and professional life. But Rosie manages to balance being an ambitious editor and a supportive best friend.

Her family had moved from the UK to Abu Dhabi when she was about fifteen years old. She was my first experience of all things British. I moved here, straight from South Africa. All I knew about the UK at the time was everything I'd read and watched in the Harry Potter series. So not much. Last time I checked; Hogwarts wasn't real. Sadly.

The difficult thing about being an expat is the constant change in your friendships. Many leave eventually, going back to their home countries to study or for family reasons. But Rosie stayed. She settled here, met a fellow Brit, and got married. Rosie is a woman who knows what she wants. Obviously, I supported her, for my own selfish reasons.

My phone buzzes on the table. I check the caller ID. Speak of the devil…

"Hey, Rosie. Shouldn't you be asleep?"

"Shouldn't you?"

"Inspiration struck me at an odd time," I say, proud of myself for staying ahead of my writing schedule. I glance at my colourful wall calendar. "Why are you awake?"

"I've been tossing and turning for the past three hours. I wish this baby would just come already," she groans.

"It's almost time," I say, trying to sound as comforting as I can. I look over to the red circle around Rosie's due date. "Speaking of which, did you get a chance to ask who your replacement will be while you're on leave?"

"Ah yes, that's what I called about."

"Now?"

"Yes."

"How did you know I was awake?"

"Your 'last seen' on WhatsApp."

"Of course. Stalker." I giggle.

"I call it research. Now, back to your new editor. He is new to *Arabian Tales*, from the States. He's flying to Abu Dhabi one of these days."

"Great," I say, deadpan.

"Try to not sound so enthusiastic when we meet him on Monday, OK?"

"I'll be fine," I lie. I will not be fine. At least, until I'm sure he is as good as Rosie. Which will be never. Probably.

"OK, I am going to attempt to get some sleep, I will chat to you later, love."

"Goodnight," I say, my voice low and weak as she clicks off.

I slide open the balcony door and step outside to clear my mind before bed. The air wraps around me like a warm, wet towel. It's a moonless night with only a hint of a breeze—typical summer weather. I hear the waves crashing lazily against the shore. The air is still salty even if I don't have a sea view. A sea view would have cost me all my limbs.

My father's voice rings in my ears. "You don't need to pay an extra fifty thousand dirhams in rent just to look at the beach when you wake up." I could not agree less, of course. He'd said it about ten times in the twenty minutes that we'd looked at the apartment, loud enough for the estate agent to hear and smile each time, twitching his brow. Many would argue that a sea view *is* worth every penny, but to my father, you could get the same view for much less by walking down to the beach. Not the same, Dad. Not. The. Same.

Much to the agent's relief, I took the apartment with the view of the apartments that will have a sea view when they're eventually built. For the moment, I have a view of the lights around the construction site in front of me.

"A new editor," I mutter. Will he like my work? He'll probably tell me that 'horror' was a genre full of clichés, and I'll have to convince him that my stories are different. Then he'll say that if I were truly good, I would already be a bestseller. He'll be right though, won't he? I shake my head to get rid of the doubt building up in my mind. I always do this to myself.

I have four published books locally and I'm known in the UAE. But I still have imposter syndrome—I just don't feel like I belong. I also work part-time for Arabian Tales, the publishing house that published my books—the part-time work helps pay the rent since the books aren't exactly flying off the shelves.

To me, a successful author needed to be on *The New York Times* bestselling list. And that's what I'm aiming to achieve with my next book. It's going to be my masterpiece. Rosie and I have worked it all out. But…. now I have a new editor.

I take another deep breath and walk back into my cool room. I climb into bed, picking up my phone to make sure the alarm is on. A new message from Rosie came through while I was outside:

Waters broke. On my way to the hospital. Wish me luck.

I smirk. Her wish had come true. Which meant I had to meet my new editor on my own. Dread washes away the little excitement I have left in me.

I close my heavy eyes.

They immediately spring open again. A screeching sound is coming from next door. I know number 245 to be empty. I squint as if that will make me hear better and search the darkness in the room. There's that sound again.

Maybe I'm just imagining it. Although, I do write 'horror novels' for a living and when you write horror, you 'hear' sounds in everything.

Unable to shake the feeling that a lost *Bedouin soul* is occupying the apartment next door, I get out of bed. As I tiptoe closer to my room wall to listen for more sounds, incidentally going against everything I insist my characters stand for, the next-door balcony light goes on. Creeping toward the door, trying to be discreet as possible so as not to disturb the restless *Bedouin ghost*, I slide my door open and peek outside.

I sigh with relief to see a real person. A man. An attractive man, is on the balcony, dragging a large bag of something which seems heavy. I jerk my head back behind the door. Is it a body? My heart jumps into my throat. I need more information. Handsome people can be killers, too. I've watched *American Psycho*.

I peep around the door again, my eyes scanning his balcony for more clues. In one corner, stand empty plant pots of various shapes and sizes. Probably his weapon of choice. It would be quite original. A small shovel standing upright next to it. On the floor, barely visible from where I'm standing, is a big black bag, narrow and long. He walks back into the apartment. This is my chance to get a closer look, so I step forward.

My shoe catches as I creep across the threshold. Luckily, I catch myself before completely tripping over. Literally falling for my handsome neighbour… Imagine that!

Still focusing on the black bag, I inch a bit closer.

"Are you spying on me?" he asks, suddenly appearing in the light.

I straighten up, realising I'm posing in a weird half-spy, half-robber stance.

I clear my throat. "Guilty," I say, putting my hands up. My eyes flash to the black bag. He catches the glance and then steps aside to look at the bag.

"Everything OK?" he asks, creases folding around his eyes.

"Uhm, yeah, I just wanted to read what's written on that black bag," I say, unable to come up with any other normal reason for standing strangely close, at one a.m., to another person's balcony railing. "Potting soil, duh!"

"What did you think it was?"

"To be honest, I thought it was a body."

This time his eyes twinkle with amusement. I'm guessing that this is the first time someone has accused him of murder.

"So…I thought the apartment was empty," I say, breaking the about-to-be awkward silence.

"Just moved in today. Sorry if I disturbed you by moving things. Trying to get everything sorted."

"No worries, I'm sorry for spying on you," I wink. "I'll leave you to it. Goodnight."

"Goodnight," he calls after me. I could feel his eyes on my back as I walk into my room.

Great. You can always rely on Diana Dawson to make a complete fool of herself.

I return to bed and close my eyes. Two changes in one day. First a new editor, and now a new neighbour. Right now I prefer the restless *Bedouin ghost.*

Chapter 2

My alarm rings at four a.m. It's Sunday. I skim through the notifications on my phone, searching for any updates from Rosie. I tap a message to check in with her, then scramble out of bed.

After a quick basin-wash, I lather my arms and hands with sunblock, with a sun protection factor of 50. Turning around in front of the mirror, I make sure that it's evenly applied up to my shoulders. Then I grab my SPF 100 and massage blobs of cream on to my face and neck. I draw closer to the mirror to check that the cream has reached all parts of my hairline. Finally, with another bottle of sun cream, this time a measly SPF of 30, I rub the cream onto the exposed parts of my shins and ankles. Now, I'm ready to go outside.

I leave the flat, pulling the door behind me. Residing in Abu Dhabi has its advantages. For instance, it is the safest city in the world according to the World Safety Index: my parents' most important selling point when anyone asks how life is in the UAE.

My parents, both teachers, moved here twenty years ago, from South Africa. I was nine, and I was not pleased to leave my best friends to make a home half way across the world. They always told me it was to keep me safe, and I couldn't prove them wrong. As beautiful as the country is, South Africa's crime was increasing by the minute, and we hardly felt safe in our own homes, even though we were living behind burglar bars and electric fences. We were prisoners in our own homes, and they decided that it was no way for me and my younger brother to grow up. So, they packed up when they found the opportunity to move, and have been here since.

The warm thick air slaps my face as I leave the building. The streetlamps buzz, breaking the silence of the early hours. There's no one in sight. I shake my legs and stretch my arms and begin to jog along the pavement.

Lamps and traffic lights cast shadows on the road as I run along the roads leaving Mamsha. The sky turns from black to deep blue as I near the St Regis Hotel. A faint scent of coffee wafts through the air as I pass by. I've missed the morning staff by a few minutes.

The majestic Saadiyat villas cluster together proudly, intimidating whoever passes by. Running to the Jumeirah Hotel isn't on the cards today—the sun is already too high in the sky.

While I'm running, my mind sometimes wanders: what would my life be like if I lived in one of those marvellous villas? An image of me lying on a sunbed, outside, next to the pool, wearing a large sunhat and sipping a martini, pops into my head. Pfft. Me? In the sun? No way.

Today I can't get my handsome neighbour out of my head. I replay our short conversation in my head, repeatedly, looking for nuances in each word and expression, but in the end, I conclude he'll primarily be concerned that his neighbour is a crazy lady who spies on others and comes up with ridiculous theories about them—at roughly one o'clock in the morning.

As I near my building, my neck and chest begin to tingle as the early sun's rays hit me. I glance at my Fitbit…

I hurry into the building, nodding to the night guard out of habit, but he's asleep and doesn't notice me. I climb the stairs to my floor but as I reach the top, I see him. The beautiful man who is now a resident of the apartment next to mine. He strolls toward the elevators, eyes glued to his phone as he taps the screen. I step back, nearly losing my balance on the stairs. Shit. He cannot see me. I inspect my hands and arms—they are slightly red but the tingling sensation has thankfully passed. I hide behind the wall and close my eyes, steadying my breath. A few seconds later I peek around the corner to check if he's gone. Then, a familiar, shrill voice calls my name.

"Diana! Darling, what on earth are you doing hiding behind that wall?"

Caitlyn Connors. The head of the body corporate of the building. Girlfriend of the CEO of the company that owned the apartments in Mamsha. She makes it her business to know as much as there is to know about everybody. Whether they lived in this building or the next. Or in Abu Dhabi. No surprise she's upstairs sniffing around the new neighbour already.

Caitlyn reminds me of a group chat where only one person ever messages updating everyone on the latest news around the country. None of the information is ever helpful, and you can't mute Caitlyn, or just leave 'the group.'

She will find you, somewhere, somehow. As her long, lean legs get closer, with the golden knot at the top of her head bouncing along, I try to push myself into the wall, hoping it will absorb me, and make me disappear. She crunches up her eyebrows and wags her manicured finger at me. She is the last person I want to see. In fact, if I never see her again, my life will probably be much better. No, definitely better.

"I just—," I use my thumb to indicate I have just returned from my run.

"We missed you on Saturday. How are you feeling?" She has the voice of someone trying to hold back a laugh in their throat.

"Much better."

"You know, if your tummy aches persist, you should see my shaman. He has the best, most natural remedies. Way better than these over-the-counter things. Nothing artificial," she declares, matter-of-factly.

Oh yes, the special herbal tea from Caitlyn's shaman looks and smells incredibly similar to ordinary green tea leaves. I'd made the mistake of actually speaking to her when I'd just moved in, not knowing that being acquainted with Caitlyn obliges you to attend her weekly meditation sessions at her home or on the beach. Naturally, she serves her 'special tea' afterward. Since then I've managed to come up with a unique engagement every time I receive an invitation. I make sure each excuse sounds disgusting enough for her to gag, put up her hand to shush me and not ask any more questions.

"Oh, I should—," I try to say, but she keeps cutting me off. Which I'm used to. One thing you should know about Caitlyn is that her conversations with you are the equivalent of Shakespearean soliloquies. One-sided, long, and boring.

"Ms Brown from 232 swears that it's a magical potion and that it's cured all her aches and pains," she says, pointedly.

She drones on about her shaman on a trip to some place, a few of the neighbours, and their 'annoying habits.' Defeated, I stand there, listening for the elevator. I steal a glance at my phone. It's been a few minutes already and I can't hear the elevator over Caitlyn's voice.

"I've got to get going, Caitlyn, see you later," I interrupt. I turn on my heel, not waiting for a reply. I sigh with relief to see that my new neighbour is now gone, and I dart toward my apartment.

I shower, and my tummy grumbles. It's not grumbling for the yogurt in my fridge or the apple on my countertop. It's grumbling for something more interesting. And I'm not one to disappoint my tummy. I head to the restaurant downstairs. All of those which usually have seating areas outside have now been brought inside. No one wants to sit in the humid air during the day. I take my laptop with me. I may do some writing. Who knows?

I walk into Beach, Eat! relieved to have the cool air-conditioning wash over me.

While I pump some sanitizer onto my hand, the waiter approaches. Her eyes crinkle behind her mask as she speaks. "Good morning, madam. Welcome," she says. "Table for one?"

"Yes, please." I nod, suddenly feeling conscious of being all alone on a Sunday morning. I follow her to a small table with two chairs next to a window, cerise bougainvillea dotted with white petals drape the sides of the terracotta pot attached to it. The morning light pours in brightening up the restaurant. I have a clear view of the sparkling blue ocean, slowly, unintentionally calming my mind. I spot a few people strolling along the beach. Turns out there are some who want to be outside in the humid air.

I'm seated a few tables away from a small family happily chatting and eating their breakfast. One day. First comes love though, doesn't it?

I scan the barcode on the table to check the menu and then the waiter asks if I'd like anything to drink. I order my usual. Emirati *shakshouka* on toasted sourdough, *karak* tea, and fresh orange juice.

I'm always amazed at the way a variety of cuisines make their way onto one plate and somehow work together perfectly. Obviously, the menu is extensive, and I am *sure* that everything they make is delicious, but why would I want to try something new when I already *know* how amazing my usual order is?

As the waiter walks away, I open up my laptop. I check my emails first. I click on the unfamiliar one from Theo Evans.

Good day, Diana.

How are you?

I believe Rosana told you about me. We will be working together for the next few months.

My flight arrives this afternoon. Thought I'd settle tonight before we meet tomorrow. AT has put me up in Yas Island Grand for a month until I find a place.

Really looking forward to meeting you. Can we have
breakfast tomorrow?

Kind regards,
Theo

I take a deep breath and reply.

Hi Theo,
    I am well, thank you. I hope you are well too. Yes,
she did mention that you would be arriving.
    Is tomorrow at 10 am OK? I will meet you at your
hotel lobby.
    Looking forward to meeting you too. Have a safe
trip.

Regards,
Diana Dawson

As I hit 'send', my breakfast arrives. Chilled juice, a piping hot cup of sweet tea, and inviting-looking eggs on toast.

Belly satisfied and smiling, I get up and hurry into my building. There's no sign of my new neighbour—much to my relief. And disappointment too, to be honest.

I sit down to fill out some forms. The *Arabian Festival of Literature* is holding an upcoming writers' competition in nine months. Rosie and I have been eyeing this opportunity for more exposure as an author. But, apparently, other people don't fill out their entrance forms nine months before the competition. Rosie always teases me for being over prepared.

Oh, Rosie! I grab my phone. A text from Rosie has come through. It's a birth announcement. I dial and wait, counting the number of pages the form has. Eventually, she picks up.

"Hey Di," she says, in between yawns.

"Congratulations," I sing. I tap the phone to change it to the loudspeaker and then go on to share the announcement on all my social media accounts. The thought of being an aunt makes me beam.

"I'm going to be a terrible Mum."

"I know. I told you not to do it. James is in trouble."

She laughs. "Di! I'm serious. She's a precious angel and I'm going to ruin her."

"I tried to warn you, Rose," I say, keeping my voice as serious as possible.

"You're not making me feel any better. You're supposed to say, "You're going to be a fantastic mom and a complete natural, Rosie, you've got this!" She says with fake conviction in her voice.

"You want me to lie?" I press my lips together, trying not to laugh.

She laughs again. And then fake cries.

"Rosie, you are going to be fine. It's only been a few hours."

"I haven't read any of the books you sent me about parenting," she admits.

I think back to the gift basket of books I gave her instead of the South African *biltong* that she had been craving. I flinch. I was lucky not to have taken a book to the head that day.

"Oh, don't worry. I also told James to read them."

"I guess that explains why he knows way too much about the colour of baby poop."

"Yikes, I hope I didn't ruin your husband."

"Nah, you've made him very efficient."

"You're welcome," I smile.

"So, what's up?"

"I'm filling in the forms."

"Now? You have like," she pauses, to check the date, I assume. "……. You have, like, nine months."

"I can get these forms out of the way, and continue with my writing—"

"How many chapters have you written for the competition?" Editor Rosie comes to the conversation.

"Twenty," I mumble.

"Twenty?" She screams into the phone. "You only need ten!"

"OK, OK, calm down, I'm not going to submit twenty chapters, I just couldn't make my mind up about which part of the story I want to submit," I say calmly.

"I don't even know why I'm surprised. Anyways, I was thinking, I'm going to be on leave for a while, so I think Theo should edit your work for the competition."

My heart flips. We had discussed his working on the book with me just so we could stay on schedule but not actually guiding me through the competition.

Rosie picks up my silence.

"Di? Are you there?"

"Yes, yes, sorry, just taking it in… I wasn't expecting him to be a permanent replacement," I say, my voice shaking.

"Your competition needs full attention. He will be perfect. And he won't be biased," she jokes. Best Friend Rosie had broken through.

I sigh and stay silent.

Sensing the discomfort in my sigh, Rosie says, "He is good, Diana, you don't have anything to worry about. I've got to go though; Sonia is back from her checkup. Chat later?"

"Yeah, bye Rosie," I say as cheerfully as I can.

I grab my pen. A slight heaviness fills my chest as I fill out my personal information. Images of the new editor grabbing my laptop out of my hands and throwing it into the ocean whirls around in my mind.

I flop on to my bed. Dread fills my stomach and works its way up to my chest.

Chapter 3

I shower and lather my body with different levels of SPF, taking care to get all the little nooks and crannies that can cause a flareup. It's a good thing I had decided against a run this morning. I don't need a red itchy rash to add discomfort to the growing knot in my stomach.

The thing is, I'm allergic to the sun. I have to wear sunblock on every bit of exposed skin, or it turns red, erupts in mini bumps all over, and on a really bad day, swells too. Luckily, it's only direct sunlight that affects me, so I'm safe before sunrise and after sunset. I have a bunch of antihistamines to help—which I need often—because when you live in the desert, it can be difficult to avoid the sun.

My allergy has unfortunately made some people—especially romantic prospects—distance themselves from me.

Like Josh Thompson from high school who stumbled backward gagging at the sight of me at our year 8 beach breakfast. I had just been diagnosed with the sun allergy and my mom accidentally bought the wrong SPF. I figured it would work and used it anyway until I was turning red, my hands and neck swelling. Josh began backing away from me as if I was going to turn into some sort of giant red monster and eat him. We were alone because I think we both wanted a first kiss moment. No kiss happened but he was kind enough to keep the sight to himself, and never made eye contact with me until we graduated from high school.

Then there was William Crawford, Rosie's university classmate. After I published my first novel, Rosie set me up with him. We went on a few dates, and I thought things were going well. He seemed like a mature guy, and we genuinely had a great time. And I had not yet ruined any of my dates with my allergy… then one night I decided to come clean. The colour drained from his face, and he gulped as if I had literally given him a bitter pill to swallow. He tried to sound concerned and interested in whether there was a cure or not, but then he scrambled out of my house, and the morning after, he dumped me, by text.

I run a brush through my hair and tint my lips with a shade of pink. I smile at myself in the mirror and introduce myself a few times, trying out different intonations: "Hi, I'm Diana."

Exasperated, I make myself a cup of coffee. I book an Uber while I wait for it to cool. Then, as each sip rejuvenates my mind and body, I scroll through social media.

I pack and repack my bag. My laptop—which I take everywhere—I value more than my phone. I'm lying. I'd better not forget my phone. And an extra tube of sunscreen lotion. I throw in more wet wipes, another bottle of hand sanitizer, and my sunglasses. I'm good to go. My phone buzzes, letting me know that the driver has arrived.

I hurry down the paved walkway to the meeting point. I pull on my mask and as I climb into the black Lexus, I'm thankful for a wave of cool air that covers me like a cloak.

At nine-fifty a.m. I'm in the Yas Island Grand hotel, a few minutes away from the waterfront called Yas Bay—a space known for its contemporary restaurants and art, modern sculptures, and futuristic designs. I'm shown to the seating area in the lobby of the hotel by a friendly-faced doorman. After he walks away, I admire the hues of grey and blue, which imitate the changing features of waves and the ocean.

Receptionists tap on keyboards as they check tourists in; concierge staff move bronze trolleys piled with luggage either toward the elevator or toward the arriving valet-driven vehicles.

The lobby is bright and spacious. It gives me the impression that the decorators wanted to recreate a breath of fresh air— but indoors. And they've succeeded. I take a few pictures for the 'gram and post them as a story on my account, tagging the hotel with the label 'workspace for the day' in blue swirly writing. As soon as I posted, a tall, slim guy in a charcoal-grey suit, and matching tie, catches my eye. I follow his stroll toward the reception area. The lower part of his face is covered in a black face mask but his eyes are focused. He must be the manager here… His dark hair looks as if it's made out of clay, firm against his head, not threatening to move from its place. Not bad.

I make a mental note to ask for the manager the next time I visit here. I chuckle to myself as I pull my phone out and sit back in my seat. As if I'll be that brave. I check the number of views I receive on the story I had posted only seconds ago. Rather to my disappointment, there are none. Oh well…

"Hello," says a deep voice.

I look up, focusing on the speaker's eyes, the colour of stormy clouds.

"I… I was just waiting for…" I stammer.

"Are you Diana?" He asks, with a distinctly American twang.

He's the editor!

I stand up and smooth down my dress. "Hello. Yes, I'm Diana Dawson," I splutter. I hold out my hand, as his smooth, cool hand takes mine.

"I'm Theo," he says. He scans me from head to toe.

"Is something wrong?" I ask as if I don't know exactly what's going through his mind.

"Rosie said you're from South Africa…" He is looking at me as if Rosie and I cooked up a plan to play a sick joke on him.

"Yes, I am. Cape Town, actually," I add.

"But where are you really from?"

I've had this conversation many many times. The Caucasian person says she's from South Africa. All they hear is the word 'Africa' and they expect you to be covered in animal skins and have a pet lion. "From South Africa," I say, jutting out my chin.

There's an awkward silence. He sighs, as if under the impression that I don't want to tell him where I'm actually from. I'm enjoying this a bit too much.

"Anyway," he continues, "…shall we get to breakfast?" His eyes crinkle, so I assume he's smiling.

I start toward the door leading out of the hotel, and he calls, "Diana, we'll have breakfast here."

I turn around and follow him to the restaurant. Or not? We walk past all the restaurants I can see. Oh well, maybe there's something on the beach. I didn't know there was a beach here. Luckily I'm wearing my summery yellow and white stripy dress.

I didn't know that there's a beach here because there is no beach. Instead, I find myself seated in a cold, poorly-lit conference room.

"I booked us a meeting room, with breakfast," he says, as he notices me scrutinising the surroundings. "I didn't know the protocol here."

A small corner of the large glass table is set. Two cups and saucers, a pot of coffee. A few croissants, which I can tell are cold, a random beaker of olive oil, and little blocks of butter and pots of jam piled into a basket and plates. And a…

"*Shisha*," I exclaim, wrinkling my brow at the smoking tobacco escaping the lit hookah pot.

"I didn't know if that was mandatory when they offered…," he says sheepishly with an apologetic raise of his hand.

I shake my head but don't make too much of a scene not wanting to embarrass him further. I must say, management must be brave for offering *shisha* indoors. Had they not thought the idea through?

I pull my laptop out of my bag and he does the same, ignoring the spread. He doesn't appear impressed by the 'breakfast' either. Someone needs to speak to the manager here. The actual manager.

He pours himself some coffee and offers to pour mine, which I accept.

He unbuttons his suit jacket and sits down, his white shirt stretching across his chest, and removes his mask. His skin is tanned, set jaw, and teeth that aren't perfectly straight. There's a day-old stubble on his face and his eyelashes are long.

"So, Diana, have you been here in Abu Dhabi for a long time?" he asks, jolting me from eyeing his every feature.

"Yeah, it's been twenty years already. We moved when I was nine."

He gives a small laugh. "Forgive me, I don't know much about South Africa. I hear the word Africa and expect you to be…" … he trails off, shifting in his seat.

"To be African," I tease.

"And have a pet lion," he adds.

"Maybe I do," I smirk.

His lips just barely move, his ears flushing red.

"So is this your first time in Abu Dhabi? Or the UAE?"

"I've been to Dubai once before, a few years ago with my girlfriend."

"Are you guys here together now?"

Theo shakes his head. "She has a great job back home, I just needed a change, and the money is better too."

"But it's only three months," I say.

Theo hesitates. He leans back in his chair and lets out a breath of air, "I'm sure that they have other projects for me."

I sip on the coffee. It's tepid and bitter, and I instantly regret it. I try to ignore his hesitation, but I'm suddenly on edge.

"So, have you heard about the Arabian Festival of Literature?"

"Not much, I'm afraid. Rosie mentioned it, but we didn't go into details."

I sit upright in my seat, ready to explain everything. "OK, well, Emirates Airline holds it every year. My life practically revolves around it. People from all over the world come to celebrate literature. You get to meet famous authors, and attend workshops and debates."

Excitement builds up in me as I explain it to Theo. "It's the largest of its kind in the Middle East. And I always plan my visit around the guest authors and their workshops or readings. Last year they had Jamie Patrick! Jamie frigging Patrick."

Theo's eyes twinkle, his mouth curving ever so slightly.

"What's wrong?"

"You seem really excited."

"I am really excited. That's not even the best part. This year, they are holding a writing competition. The airline will be sponsoring the prize as well. A month-long book tour in the US!" I almost jump out of my chair.

Trying to steady my voice again, I say quietly, "The prize will give any upcoming author international recognition."

Forgetting how terrible the coffee is, I take another sip, attempting to calm my nerves.

"And you're entering the competition?" Theo asks.

"I am. Rosie suggested I give it a shot. The novel I'm working on now is the one I'm going to submit," I smile.

"No pressure," Theo jokes.

"Yeah, no pressure."

We come up with a schedule for the next month, trying to align our calendars.

"So, were you an editor in the US?" I ask.

"No, actually, I was an English teacher. I taught middle school, grades six to eight." He pauses as if he's traveling back to a good memory. "I miss those brats," he adds a moment later.

"How did you get into editing?"

"I used to do some freelance work for a company my girlfriend works for." He remains silent for a while. I surmise that anything related to his girlfriend is a touchy subject.

"So, why the UAE?" I ask with a slight cough. The tobacco is getting to my throat.

"This job came up and I thought it would be an adventure. I have a few friends here. They love it here and know others from back home who love it too. I'm curious to know what made the UAE so desirable to everyone."

"I'm sure you will love it here." I begin coughing again.

"I probably should put this thing out," says Theo, standing over the *Shisha* apparatus. He fiddles around without much success. I'm about to pass a helpful suggestion when he lifts the metal dish with the coals. I wince and watch as a horrified expression fills his face.

"Ouch!" he yells, dropping the dish. Burning coals spill across the table. A piece must have fallen into the olive oil because it goes up in flames.

We both reactively grab at it, our hands colliding, knocking it over and setting alight napkins, butter, and a bunch of marketing pamphlets.

Suddenly, the fire alarm goes off.

"Let's get help!" I shout over the blaring sound, grabbing my laptop and shoving it into my bag. We both hurriedly pack our things, not a moment too soon.

The sprinklers from the roof, switch on and a shower of water drenches us. A hotel assistant flings open the door assesses the situation in seconds and rushes out. We run for the open doors, nearly bumping into him as he rushes back carrying a fire extinguisher.

We turn to watch as he opens it up with a whoosh over the flames lathering the table with white, gooey foam.

I sigh in relief.

"We're really, sorry," Theo begins. "We're…"

"No problem, ma'am, sir," he says. Picking up his walkie-talkie, he radios in, "Fire is out. Situation is under control. I repeat. Situation is under control. Cancel evacuation."

As we both continue to blurt apologies to him, we hear over the intercom, that it's a false alarm followed by instructions for all guests to return to their rooms.

The assistant takes us by the elbows with a smile and firmly guides us out of the room.

"Don't worry; everything is under control," he says tightlipped. "You can go now."

I follow Theo to the closest elevator, conscious that my drenched dress is clinging to my body. He invites me to come to his room to dry up and I don't refuse.

Cold beads of water drip from my hair and dribble down my back sending a shiver through me. The hallway down to his room is an extension of the decor in the lobby, without the breezy feeling, but still relatively bright and modern in shades of blue. He pulls out his key card from his wet pocket with some difficulty and opens the door.

I enter the little foyer of his suite and walk straight to the oak dining-room table where I place my bag on one of the quilted dining-room chairs. I notice washed dishes in the sink of the fully-fitted kitchen. Did he cook his own food last night?

As if reading my thoughts, Theo says, "I made dinner for myself last night."

"Ah, he cooks," I reply.

He looks down at his feet and chuckles. "A guy's got to eat."

"Is it a hobby?" I say, mildly impressed. I couldn't really say the same about myself. I live alone and usually go out to eat with friends and family. I bite my lip.

"Nah, I just cook for survival," he says casually as if knowing exactly what I'm thinking. "I could teach you," he offers.

"You'd be wasting your time. I can burn ice."

Theo grins, shaking his head.

"I should probably go home; I don't have any clothes," I say, looking down at my wet clothes.

"No, don't, there is a shower in the second bedroom. I'll use the one in my room." He points to his room in the far right corner.

We walk together to the bathroom. He opens the door and switches on the lights.

"Take your time," he says, "I'll bring you some of my clothes."

I thank him and he smiles before giving me some privacy.

I enter the warmly-lit bathroom and the first thing I notice is my dishevelled appearance in the mirror. My hair has completely frizzed up! I strip off my clothing, hanging everything on the freestanding bathtub with rustic gold fittings. I step into the shower, sighing with relief at the comforting warmth as I wipe away my makeup. Luckily for me, there's complimentary shampoo and conditioner that I can use to repair some of the damage to my unruly mane.

I close the tap and come out, covering myself with the towelling gown. When I enter the room, on the bed lies a set of navy-blue men's pyjamas.

After rubbing sun-cream all over my body, I pull on the pyjamas and roll up the waist of the pants. I take out the hairdryer from the nightstand and dry my hair, running my fingers through it, doing my best to tame it.

I return to the dining room and gather my hair into a pony-tail with a hairband from my bag. I glance at my reflection in the mirror on the wall. Staring back is an image of a rather ill-looking nine-year-old girl. No makeup, extra-large pyjamas. Rosie will have a laugh at this. I take my phone out of my bag and snap a selfie.

Just as I click, Theo walks in.

His hair has retained its sculpted look, but his face is shaven. He's wearing dark blue denim and a white T-shirt that's hanging loosely on his body.

"A selfie in your designer pyjamas?" he asks, his eyebrows knitting.

"Haa," I say. "I'm sending it to Rosie, updating her on our first meeting."

"It will definitely be memorable," he replies, gesturing to a chair near the kitchen island. "Let me make a real breakfast for you."

Watching him cook is like watching an artist. He's moving swiftly and smoothly, dicing red onions, slicing cherry tomatoes and button mushrooms, and grating cheese. After adding a blob of butter, which sizzles in the hot pan, he whisks the eggs, adds a splash of milk then adds the veggies to the pan—they steam and splutter, sending a delicious aroma throughout the room.

My stomach grumbles. He is so focused on what he is doing. Surely, he hasn't forgotten that I'm here? Maybe I can just pretend to be busy with something, too? I scroll aimlessly through my social media and check to see if Rosie has replied. No, she hasn't. Would it be weird if I took out my laptop and did some work? My fingers are searching for something to do…

"Can I lay the table?" I ask, my voice raised slightly.

"Oh yeah, sure, the plates are over there," he points to a cupboard next to the fridge. "And there's orange juice in the fridge as well, if you don't mind."

"Not at all," I smile, glad to finally have something to do.

I carry the plates to the kitchen island while Theo adds the eggs to his frying pan and finally puts a tortilla on top. I pour the juice into glasses I find in the same cupboard.

He rolls up the tortilla in the frying pan and slices it in half, placing a piece on each of our plates. We both take our seats.

Noticing the impressed look on my face, he says, "I hope you were taking notes, Diana."

"I made mental notes," I wink and sink my teeth into the breakfast burrito. We eat quietly.

Rosie is right. He is a good editor. She never cooks for me.

****

My phone buzzes as I enter my apartment. Trust Rosie to want an update immediately.

"So? How did it go?" she asks, her voice much higher in pitch than usual.

"Went well actually, given how things started off. They popped some tables and chairs in a dungeon and called it a conference room…"

She laughs. "I am sure it was not that bad."

"I felt like I was being called in for interrogation by the FBI. Then there was a fire, and the sprays went on and drenched us."

"What?"

"Yeah, then we went back to his suite and the rest was history."

"Could you not be so cryptic?"

I laugh and relay the whole day for Rosie.

I go to bed early that night. It's a hot but peaceful night. The usual crash of the waves lulls me to sleep.

Chapter 4

I run as fast as I can, my skin on fire, itching as if a million ants are crawling all over my body with their tiny little legs. My heart bangs loudly against my rib cage, trying to escape, and my lungs are burning. While I'm used to this feeling, it's not something I enjoy I must admit… I finally make it up the stairs but my legs are getting heavier and heavier, and struggling to carry me. I fumble for my house key, droplets of sweat running down my head, making my face itch even more. I push the door open and shut it behind me.

I wobble over to my medicine cabinet and yank it open, my eyes darting around for the pill that will give me instant relief. I open the bottle clumsily and gulp down the pills, letting the cool water dribble down my scorching face and neck, providing temporary relief from the overactive ants. A moment later my body slowly cools down, the ants hurrying away, until another day.

My skin will be blotchy and slightly swollen for the next few hours, but luckily I'm at home.

I bask in the cool AC air, browsing through my social feeds, when suddenly the doorbell rings. I jerk my head. I'm not expecting any deliveries today— as far as I can remember. I remove my sneakers and tiptoe to the front door. I peek into the eye hole and my heart immediately somersaults.

Shit. It's the surfer guy, from next door. OK, I am only assuming that he surfs from the beachy hair and boardshorts, and the tie-dye T-shirt that had "Do you even surf bro?" sprawled across it. I didn't get a good enough look at him the other night anyway. But, in my mind, he surfs.

This is not how our first official meeting should go.

Men in my past have always reacted badly when they saw me after an allergic reaction. Some gagged in front of me. Some just backed away, fearing they would catch my 'disease.' I really don't think it's that bad, but some people are so tied to the idea of perfection, that anything out of that range is too much for them to handle.

I can't let him see me like this—red, blotchy, and severely uncomfortable in my own skin. I run to the coat cupboard and pull on the first thing that catches my eye. Anything to keep him from thinking I turn into a giant red starfish overnight.

I take a breath and swing the door open. "Hi," I say, trying to sound casual, my voice slightly muffled.

Surfer guy's eyes widen and a small space forms between his lips. His eyes rake in the sight before him, from head to toe, clearly not having expected to see what's in front of him. He blinks, realising his face was frozen for a split second.

Covered from head to toe in a puffy yellow garment with a transparent plastic sheet covering the face, I stand waiting for his response. I slipped on my fluffy white bunny slippers as well, but my hands are bare—thankfully they aren't red.

"You're wearing a hazmat suit." He gulps, then squeezes his lips together. He finally clears his throat.

"Yes… I was… uhm… trying it on. The whole pandemic made me quite paranoid, you know. And I thought I would check if it fits, just in case there's another new super contagious variant around," I explain, trying to keep my voice steady and convincing.

He nods. "I see," he drawls. "If you happen to have a spare one lying around, I wouldn't mind taking it off your hands." With a straight face, he continues, "You know—just in case there's another super contagious variant around."

I breathe out an exasperated laugh, and reply, "Of course."

Surfer guy winks at me. Shit, I need to remember to not call him that out loud.

"I was coming over to introduce myself a bit more formally…after the other night… I'm Lucas, by the way."

"Diana. And, welcome to the building… Um…." I shot a glance down at my attire, I can't invite him in while I look like I am about to clean up some sort of toxic spill. There are a hundred things that I want to ask him, but right now I'm beginning to cook inside this suit.

"Great," he says, probably catching my glance. "Should I come back later?"

"Yes!" I practically scream. *Please do.*

He smiles and walks away. I close the door, sighing with relief as I lift off the hat. I look in the mirror—my cheeks are flushed; my heart is pounding against my ribcage once more. That was close.

On the one hand, Lucas won't think I'm a red starfish. On the other hand, he probably thinks that I am seriously whacky.

Lucas could live in my mind *rent-free*. I chuckle to myself at my little joke. While the hot spray of the shower hits my face, I close my eyes and his deep voice rings in my ear. As I dry off and slip into my loungewear, I think about the black T-shirt that clung, almost possessively, to every curve of his physique. While I dry my hair I think about his luscious locks—which are the colour of the sunkissed Arabian desert sand. Stirring my coffee, I think about the manicured beard that covers his face but still allows his impressive jawline to show through.

I sit down at my laptop and think about Lucas' piercing blue eyes that can put the ocean of Saadiyat Island to shame. His eyes are as inviting as the turquoise waters of the beach behind me, and they could well enough peer into my soul if it hadn't been for my hazmat suit.

I stand back up again. I pace the living room. I switch the kettle on. The water boils while I take out a cup from the cupboard. I pace the living room some more, biting my nail, biting my sleeve. I boil the kettle again, and while the water boils I take out a teabag. Hmm… maybe chamomile would help calm my nerves. What does he mean by, "Should I come back later?" Did he mean tonight? Or this afternoon?

I look at the clock; it's noon. Will Lucas wait a few days before he visits again? Or, maybe, he won't return at all. And what does he expect when he comes by in the first place? The questions swirl around in my mind. Is he just being polite? It was probably that, right? OK, so I guess he isn't coming back. Which I'm fine with. I guess.

No, I am not. I have got to find a way to bump into him. Completely by chance of course. Purely coincidental.

I sit down at my laptop again and type into the Google search engine: "How to bump into your crush on purpose." I have to say, I am pleasantly surprised at the number of articles that have actually come up. I scan an article by Cosmo—completely pointless, more like an excerpt from a romance novel. I'm not interested in a story—just the rules. There's another article about someone trying to bump into their crush on purpose and it did not work out. I'm not reading that article—I don't need that kind of negativity in my life. Finally, I click on the article I'm looking for—the internet never ceases to amaze me—" How to accidentally bump into a guy.

" *The best way to handle your desire to bump into your crush is to be at some of the same places already.*" That one's easy—he's my neighbour, after all. "*Figure out what you and your crush have in common, and then make an effort to pursue that interest more actively in the hopes that you'll be in the same place at the same time.*" Now this one is a bit tricky. I've only met him once. Is there a way to find out about his interests without speaking to him? The article has a four-step plan:

Step 1: ask about his interests

Step 2: attend his local hangouts with his friends

Step 3: befriend his friends

Step 4: talk to him

Sounds simple enough.

Chapter 5

Jamie pushed the wooden door open. It was rough under her fingers and creaked as it swung inward. The dim light cast shadows on the walls. They both walk in, Jamie holding the knife in front of her and Isabella, with a wooden plank raised in a ready baseball hitter position. They breathed in relief; the cabin was empty, but there was a low fire in the hearth. The room was warm; there was a lamp on the small wooden table in front of them. A worn-out suede couch lay in the corner, a makeshift bed it seemed, a pillow squashed in, and a tattered blanket roughly folded on the armrest. A few metal plates and cups lay in the sink. The girls took in everything in the room as if the furniture would give them the answers they were looking for.

My phone buzzes. I tap my screen and it lights up. There's a WhatsApp banner across the screen and I read the message without opening the app.

```
Hey, hope you don't mind that I asked Caitlyn for
your phone number. Lucas.
```

I don't open the app immediately because… Seriously, I'm a modern, independent woman—I can't be giving the impression that I'm totally available and that I don't have anything else to do but hang around my phone waiting for someone to text me. I stare at the message for a moment trying to think of the best reply.

Hey Lucas, no problem, I really thought I scared you off yesterday so it's good to hear from you. *No, I shouldn't give him any indication that I thought about that incident the entire day and night.*

Hey Lucas, please try to avoid further contact with Caitlyn else she will rope you into her meditation group and fill you up with her shaman's 'special tea.' *No, Diana, don't be a gossip.*

Hey Lucas, great to hear from you, of course, I don't mind. *That seems casual enough.*

I finally open WhatsApp and type:

Hey, of course, I don't mind. 😊

I hit 'send' and that's it. Nothing to read between the lines.

Theo is coming over today. Since I don't have an office or my spectacular vision board set up there, I'll just have to take him through everything here.

The doorbell rings.

"Hey," I smile as I open the door.

Theo is wearing a navy-blue suit which is perfectly tailored. To my apartment. He must be really dedicated to his job.

"Good morning." He holds up a brown Starbucks takeaway bag. "I brought breakfast."

"Unacceptable. How dare you bring me breakfast that you haven't prepared with your own hands?" I shake my head. "This is your last chance," I joke, lifting my chin.

I take the bag from Theo, and he comes inside.

"You can leave your stuff on the dining room table; we'll work there," I say, gesturing to the table with one hand while pulling out the coffee cups and fruit parfaits from the brown bag. The delicious aroma of coffee fills the living area.

Theo leaves his laptop and phone on the table. He takes a quick walk around the living area. "Nice place," he says.

"Thank you," I smile. I place the food and drinks on a tray and bring it to the table.

He walks up to my vision board, which from here, looks quite chaotic. Much like my mind at most times, I must admit. I scan his face. He seems to be studying everything written on the colourful notes. He lifts his eyebrows. "I'm thoroughly impressed and confused at the same time."

"Grab a seat, I'll explain everything to you."

Once Theo sits down, I walk to my vision board at the other end of the table. After taking a swig of hot, fresh coffee, I rub my palms. "OK, let's begin."

Theo's eyes are wide.

"I'll just recap what happened in 'The Lake house,' OK?" Theo nods.

I begin explaining the plot of 'The Lake house' to him. Theo leans forward in his chair, his gaze fixed on me while he sips his coffee every few moments.

Gulping my coffee, I continue taking Theo through Jamie and Isabella's previous journey. He asks some questions about the story in between. I sit up straight in my seat, bouncing around slightly on the edge of my seat, ready to answer and explain everything.

Theo lets out a deep sigh. "Wow. You've left your readers on quite the cliffhanger."

"Yes." I nod.

Theo stands up and joins me at the vision board. For the next twenty minutes, he mulls over the board, occasionally pointing at notes that I've made and asking about them. I scribble notes onto colourful Post-its as new ideas pop into my mind.

Eventually, Theo takes a step back.

I sit back down, leaning in my chair. I can feel Theo's eyes on me as I tuck my hair behind my ear and drain the last of my coffee. "Is something wrong?"

Theo's lips break into a soft smile. "You really love what you do. It's actually refreshing… and watching the fire in your eyes when you talk about your work…well, it's inspiring."

I smile as I open the fruit parfait and dunk my spoon into the yogurt. I can count the number of times someone called me 'inspiring' on one hand. With three fingers curled up.

Theo opens his fruit parfait too and then cocks his head. "Or scary. To be so passionate about horror." He smiles mischievously. "Why horror, by the way?"

After swallowing a spoonful of yogurt, I reply. "I've always been a fan of the horror genre. I love the feeling of suspense building up in me. But I hate all the illogical things the characters do. Why is it always a dysfunctional family with an emo teenager moving into a dilapidated house they know is haunted? Why does the youngest child somehow communicate with the evil spirits? Oh, and my least favourite, characters hearing strange noises and moving toward the sound?"

Theo shakes his head and chuckles. "That happens in probably every horror movie I've watched."

I throw my hands up in the air. "Don't these characters have any sense of self-preservation?"

"Why are they always lost without any phone signal?" Theo counters my question.

"Why are their phone batteries always dead?" I fire back.

"I'll do you one better. Why are the police, supposedly trained law enforcement, always outsmarted by a bunch of teens?"

"Exactly!" I exclaim.

We both lean back in our seats, helping ourselves to more parfait.

"So, you're rewriting horror?" Theo asks.

"Damn straight." I put my hand up, sticking out my thumb, and continue counting out on my fingers. "My characters carry charged battery packs if they're going anywhere. They know how to use Google Maps. They stay together. They…well, you get the point."

Chapter 6

It's nearly time for my meeting with Theo. In all, it's going be a ten-minute review of the work I have done so far before we head off for a desert safari. He said that he wanted to explore the city and asked if I'm free. I gladly accepted because I love showing off this country to visitors. And, it gives me a chance to get to know Theo a bit more.

I close up my laptop and take my phone off silent. Still no reply from Lucas after he texted the other day. But why should he reply? I haven't really said anything. I hope he won't think me a cold person. That'll be rather ironic, considering I literally burn up and turn red. I throw my phone into my handbag and get dressed.

After applying an extra layer of sunblock all over my body and stepping into linen pants, I pull a tank top over my head, covering my shoulders with a thin striped shawl. I spray a little 'Spray 'n' Shine' on my hair and cram my hat and sunglasses into my bag, along with an almost empty tube of sunscreen and a bottle of antihistamines. Lastly, I slip on a pair of sandals. There is no point in wearing closed shoes to a desert camp. You end up with dunes of your own in your footwear. And in your home for many days post-desert trip. I've learned this the hard way.

We arrange to meet at Starbucks in Yas Mall. The 4x4 SUV will pick us up from the meeting point there and then it'll be an hour's drive to the desert. As I walk into the crowded coffee shop, I spot Theo at a table. Neither of us has brought a laptop, so this is going to be a very casual meeting. I saved my draft brainstorm on my phone for reference.

Rosie will be proud. She always teases me about how over-prepared I am for all my meetings with her—laptops, extra printed copies of the chapters, and an extra laptop charger just in case one of our laptops died. If she were to see me walking to a 'meeting,' wearing flats and carrying a beach bag, she would probably throw a party in my honour. Or check my temperature and send me to a hospital.

Theo waves at me. He's wearing dark jeans and a charcoal grey T-shirt. He dresses down quite nicely. His hair is gelled back and his face has light stubble. I walk over to him and place my bag on the floor.

"Hey, how are you?" I smile as I sat down.

"Great, how are you?"

"I'm alright. Excited for the desert safari?"

"I don't know what I'm getting myself into, so excited wouldn't be the word I'd use," His lip curves slightly.

"You'll survive," I reassure him.

"So, what can I get you?" He stands up to leave.

"An iced latte please," I dig into my bag for my wallet. "Hold on." Unable to find my wallet, I take out my tubes of sunscreen, my bottle of antihistamines, and my hat and lay them on the table. I finally retrieve it and hand a fifty dirham note to him.

Theo's eyes widen at the pile of stuff on the table 'I think I over-packed.' He gestures to his empty seat.

I laugh. "Long story."

He glances at his watch and brushes away the money I offer him. "We have time. I'll be right back."

He strides off toward the counter and places an order. I pack everything back into my bag and look over at Theo. I can tell him I'm allergic to the sun. He won't really care and it won't bother him. It'll just be a funny story to tell his girlfriend and they'll both just sit and laugh at how unfair life is for other people. I'm totally fine with it—I'll never meet his girlfriend; his girlfriend won't know who I am. There's no need to hide it from him.

He comes back, our orders in his hand, and places them on the table.

"I'm clearly missing something," he says, looking at my bag.

I take a deep breath. "I'm allergic to the sun," I say flatly.

He raises his eyebrows. I can immediately tell what he's thinking: a person living in the desert is allergic to the sun?

Confirming my assumption, he says: "You know, there are countries where people hardly see the sun. Ever think of relocating to England or Iceland or—"

"I can't just jet off to England," I say.

"Why not?" he asks, squeezing his brows together.

"My life is here, my family is here," I say as if he's suggesting something incredibly ridiculous. Which he is. Me. Alone in England. Only see my family occasionally, and only have to deal with the sun a few weeks a year. Damn, I have to say, it all sounds very inviting all of a sudden. Why haven't I considered moving before?

"I'm not adventurous. I don't just try new things. I think about them first, make a list of the pros and cons of doing said new things; I get anxious, and then I don't do them."

He laughs, putting his hands up to surrender.

"So what happens?" he asks. I study his face for a moment. His eager gaze, the frown lines on his forehead…he seems genuinely interested. As we sip our coffees I explain everything to him. How bad my reactions can get, my treatments, and my limitations in the sun. He just listens quietly, nodding every now and then. No disgust or disdain—at least from what I can see.

My phone rings, cutting me off. The caller ID is an unknown number.

"Hello?"

A voice answers back, "Hello Madam. Your car is here, please meet me at the mall entrance next to Daiso."

"Oh all right, thank you, we will be there in a few minutes," I say into the phone.

"Our driver is here." I smile at Theo. I'm glad this conversation is over for two reasons. One, my stomach knotted as I told him, waiting for a disapproving look to come over his face. Two, I feel lighter, like a boulder has been lifted off my chest. He is one more person I don't have to hide my allergy from anymore.

We drain the last of our coffees and make our way hurriedly toward the mall entrance. Through the doors, I see an SUV parked outside with a big red sign that says *Arabian Tours* printed beneath a logo of red desert dunes and a red camel. In front of the doors, there's a small counter with a matching sign, a man shuffling behind it. I step toward it.

"Hello, I'm Diana. We're here for the desert safari."

The man turns around. He has a pin attached to his red T-shirt that says 'Joshua.' "Hello ma'am, sir," he looks down as he consults his sheets of paper. "Private tour, right?" he asks.

"Yes, for two," I reply.

He hands me a glossy pamphlet full of safety rules and other safari offers. "Welcome to *Arabian Tours*, we hope you will enjoy your experience." Theo and I say thank you in unison and smile—which would be a crinkle around the eyes to Joshua. He gestures toward the doors and starts walking in front of us.

We follow him quietly out of the mall. Once we're out, Joshua points toward a man standing upright in front of the SUV.

"Hello, I am Jai," the man calls out.

He puts his palm on his chest, then opens the back door for us. Theo and I climb into the SUV and settle down. Our driver gets in and clicks his seat belt on. He turns to us. "Is this your first time on a desert safari?"

"I've been before, many years ago… It's his first time," I say, turning toward Theo.

"OK, welcome," says the driver. "It will take about forty minutes to get out into the desert."

We both nod.

Our journey starts off in silence. The driver keeps his eyes on the road and so does Theo. His eyes widen, staring in amazement, like a five-year-old child at Disneyland. If he has any questions, he's keeping them to himself. Reading the room, or car, in this case, I too just gaze outside at the familiar sights of shopping centres, schools, and suburbs. It's hardly a tedious drive because there's always something new being built or refashioned. The constant change and development are ceaseless. Abu Dhabi is always upgrading and expanding, like its sister emirate, Dubai. A constant hub for innovation.

As we drive on, Theo occasionally poses a question about a landmark or building we're passing. I answer as best as I can, without sounding like a Wikipedia entry.

We pass most of the developed areas and find that we are nearing the empty desert with a few houses or little cafes dotted along the main road. Our driver suddenly speaks, letting us know that we should buckle up now if haven't already and that we are now going into the dunes. Theo takes a deep breath.

"Nervous?"

"No." He shakes his head. He looks excited. He rubs his palms together and says, "Let's do it."

The driver takes another left and immediately we are on the soft dunes.

Jai steadily increases his speed. In a second the car lurches forward, roaring to climb the dune, and Theo and I are flung back into our seats. Suddenly we fall forward as the car lurches down another dune. The car is going at an incredible speed, rocking and sliding. I watch Theo's reaction. His excitement has been replaced with something a bit more *I expected a Ferris wheel experience, I've got a broken roller coaster.* Not good. Another zig-zagging lurch up a dune and then, immediately, a plunge down, twisting my intestines.

"Are you OK?" I ask Theo. His knuckles are white from holding the handlebar and his forehead glistens slightly with sweat. He hasn't turned green yet. That's a good sign, I suppose.

He nods. "Uh-huh," he groans.

He's definitely not OK. I bet myself fifty dirhams that he won't survive the rest of the journey without throwing up. We zig-zag up and down dunes at incredible speeds for what feels like two hours. I glance at my phone again, trying not to bash my head into the seat in front of me. Nope, it'd only been ten minutes. Dammit. I don't think Theo is going to survive much longer. I glance at him from the corner of my eye. He's turning a ghastly shade of green. I offer him some cool water but he pushes it away, shaking his head.

"I think I need…" he gasps.

"Jai," I call out. "Do you mind if we pull over? I think Theo is going to be sick."

"OK, madam," the driver replies, and a minute later we come to a sudden halt—which I'm sure doesn't make Theo feel any better. Theo unlocks his seatbelt, jumps out of the car, and, shoves the door closed with a loud thud. Immediately, the sound of forceful retching follows. Jai jumps down as well and goes around the back of the car with some water. I owe myself fifty dirhams.

I wait for the retching to stop and then open the car door, the hot air smacking my face. I remove my sandals and walk around the front of the car. The men are chatting, while fat droplets of sweat run down Theo's face as he gingerly sips the water Jai offers him. "It happens to everyone, Mr. Theo, don't worry," he says, trying to comfort him.

As I approach him, he raises his eyes to meet mine, his face flushed.

"I'm embarrassed," he says.

I pursed my lips together, suppressing a laugh.

"Don't be. I guess the first time is hard for everyone," I shrug.

"I'd rather my first time hadn't been with you," he says.

"Excuse me?" I raise my eyebrows. OK, clearly he thinks I'm not worthy.

Noticing my expression, he laughs and says, "That came out wrong."

I blink. "Yeah?"

"Yes!" he says, trying to convince me that he's not insulting me. "I meant that I'd rather you not think of me as a wimp who can't handle a bit of sand."

"Too late, I already think you're a wimp who can't handle a bit of sand," I retort, heatedly.

After Jai repeatedly asks Theo if he's sure he can continue, we climb back into the SUV.

What did he mean when he said that he wouldn't want his first time with me? Why is this even bothering me? We are talking about dune bashing. Nothing else. It shouldn't offend me. *Obviously,* he didn't mean it *that* way because *that* would be highly inappropriate.

Jai checks if Theo is ready to continue but he says that he would prefer just to go straight to camp. Jai mentions it'll take about twenty minutes for us to reach it.

It's late afternoon, about an hour before sunset; the sun is now marigold yellow and the sky is turning burnt orange when we arrive at the camp. We get out of the car, and I remove my sandals once again. My feet sink into the warm, soft sand and I step forward, looking around the camp.

Striped black and red tents are set up in a wide circle around the camp. In some of the tents rows of low tables and long cushions lay on either side. The tables are set with white cloths and bottles of water in the middle. Some of the other tents have signs in front of them, which from my previous visits, I know are for henna and shisha. The faint scent of smoke and sweetness wafts through the air all the way from the tents.

In the middle of the camp is a large circular platform, which will be lit up and used for the night's entertainment—a *tanoura* dance and of course, belly dancing. In between the tents, BBQ stations are set up with big silver chafing dishes ready to be filled with food. On the far end, there are a few camels, resting sullenly on the sand. Two of them are walking around slowly, with people on their backs. On the opposite side, a few hundred meters away from the main camp are buggies and four-wheelers zooming all around the smaller dunes.

The air is warm but I cover my arms with my light shawl anyway. Theo walks around looking a bit pale, but his pallor is an improvement on that nasty shade of green. His hair is not perfectly gelled anymore; a single curl hung down onto his forehead. The sun alters the shade of his eyes to silver. He's breathing in deeply as if there's something about the air in the desert that isn't quite the same. Which, I suppose, is correct.

He suddenly faces me. I look away quickly as if I had not been soaking him in through my eyes. Technically, I could have been studying the bare patch of sand behind him, or admiring the camels effortlessly pulling themselves up with their two-hundred-pound human loads.

"Do you want to ride a camel?" he asks.

"Uh-huh, I was just admiring their strength," I say, nonchalantly. Just putting it out there. Just in case he thinks I'm checking him out. He'd be wrong. I'm checking the camels out. Not in a weird way. Just out of pure admiration for God's work—which includes Theo too, I suppose.

We walk over to the area where all the camels are sitting and ask the man there if we could each have a ride. We pay our twenty-five dirhams each and wait in the queue.

"I assume you're feeling better," watching colour return to Theo's face slowly.

"Yeah, thankfully, I was afraid I had ruined this evening for you,"

"Not at all, but it wouldn't have been an easy journey for you, to go back the way we came."

"I'd rather not think about it."

"So, adrenaline isn't your thing?"

"I think my body missed the memo, given I come from a family of junkies."

"Really?"

"Yeah… my dad used to take us rafting and horse-riding on weekends; it was like our family tradition. And then my parents got divorced, and to make up for his absence my mom would book skydiving or white water rafting every other weekend. And now she has an insatiable appetite for adrenaline. She's mountain climbing with friends this weekend," he says flatly, as if mountain climbing is every middle-aged woman's hobby.

I raise my eyebrows. "Wow, she seems—"

"Hardcore." He completes my sentence.

"Yes… that would be it." I giggle.

We hear the camel caretaker call us from behind. "Madam, sir, it is your turn now,"

I approach the seated camel, his back covered with a few layers of blankets. I climb up onto the prepared seat and make myself comfortable. Behind me, I hear Theo getting up and settling on the camel on instruction from the guide, all the while asking questions about camels. Once Theo is seated, the camels both begin to move and steadily rise into the air. At first, my camel lurches me forward, wobbles a bit, onto his front knees then moves upward. I turn to look at Theo, whose beautiful smile is plastered to his face. I face forward again, shaking out the silliness in my mind. He doesn't have a beautiful smile. It's ordinary. Just like the camel caretaker's toothless grin.

My body jerks with each step the camel makes along the designated path. I squint into the distance, perfect ripples of sand forming on the dunes, dark green shrubs dotted here and there. The beauty of absolutely nothing, I call it. A few minutes later the camel makes its way around and we are back to the resting area. The animal carefully sits down, once again sending me lurching forward.

The sun is now a fiery orange and the sky is turning indigo, mixed with hues of velvet reds and plum purples. More SUVs arrive, filled with people eager for the cultural festivities the night ahead holds. After Theo visits the bathroom, we find ourselves on soft cushions around the empty table near the circular platform, affording us a front-seat view of tonight's entertainment. We help ourselves to the cool water provided and sit patiently soaking in the desert ambience. The lights flash on one by one around us as the sky darkens.

Waiters bring large platters of crispy vegetable *pakoras* and herby cheese spring rolls. People from around the camp swarm toward the tent, seating themselves as close to the stage as possible. The sound of people chatting and laughing, the clatter of cutlery and the moments of silence in between, the smell of smoke and meat fills the air. Slowly people stand up, making their way to the buffet line.

Theo and I follow suit. We make our way to the queue. I pick up my warm plate and scan everything on offer. Hummus, *mutabbal*, *fattoush*, *tabouleh*, falafels, Arabic breads, parathas, skewered meat, chicken, and prawns. As we move down the buffet line, I glimpse steaming pots of sweet *umm Ali*. Next to them, ladies fry *luqaimat*, gathering golden balls of dough from the oil and immediately dropping them into bubbling date syrup, only to pile them high in little bowls. The final touch is a toothpick through the topmost ball of sweet syrupy golden dough and a light sprinkle of sesame seeds. I'll need to save space for dessert.

We make our way slowly through a hearty supper, finishing with indulgent sweet dishes while we're treated to a light show in the form of a *tanoura* dance.

I watch the man donning a high hat and a colourful multilayered skirt, twirling as fast as he can, and my head starts to spin with him as well. His feet move at such speed and he doesn't seem to lose balance. He ends with a bow and the crowd cheers and claps. Next, we hear the gentle clink of beads. As the music starts, a slim lady with long blonde hair that falls to her hips swinging gracefully from side to side, strides on to the stage. She moves her body to the music as the jewels and mini golden coins sewed to her vibrant pink skirt and top jingle along with her. The men whistle and the women glare at the men who whistle. I shoot a glance at Theo. He's quite taken with the beauty in front of him as well.

I nudge him with a grin and he blushes. A moment later, the belly dancer clinks on over, holding her hands out to Theo. Around us, the audience claps loudly, encouraging him. He glances at me, trying to hide the excitement that spread across his face. I nod, with slight envy.

"Come, dance weeth me," the dancer says in a thick Russian accent.

Theo stands up and follows her onto the stage. She gestures to him to follow her dance moves and Theo gives them his best effort. I laugh until my stomach hurts. A lady at the table next to mine nudges me. "Your boyfriend is a good dancer," her voice strains over the loud music and noisy audience. I try to scream back at her, "He's not my boyfriend," but my voice is drowned out by a loud cheer from the audience as the belly dancer and Theo bow.

Theo settles back into his seat, breathing heavily, face glistening. After he gulps down some water, he speaks between huffs of breath. "That was the most fun I've had in a while."

"It was quite a sight." I grin.

I meet his gaze. His eyes are softer than usual, more welcoming. I quickly avert my eyes, turning my attention to the couples who get up to swirl around with the slow music.

When the festivities are over, we walk back to our SUV, our feet sinking into the cool sand with each step.

"Thanks for coming with me tonight," Theo says, glancing at me, his lips split into a smile. "I had fun."

"No problem, I'm glad you enjoyed…. most of it." I smile back.

The driver drops us off at Yas Mall. From there, Theo heads to his hotel and I jump into a taxi back home.

****

My legs feel like cement as I trudge into a warm shower. My bed welcomes me with open arms. With heavy eyes, I check my unread messages. I gasp. Lucas has messaged.

I open his message.

```
Hey Diana, I was wondering if you would like to hang
out one of these days. Let me know. 😊
```

I reply immediately.

```
What do you have in mind?
```

Under his name, it shows 'typing…' in green writing. His reply comes the next moment.

```
How do you feel about jet skiing? And we can grab a
coffee afterward.
```

My eyes widen and my chest drops. Jet skiing? Out in the sun without a covering. Absolutely not. But…he is asking me out. It's not a date… but what if I say no and completely ruin my chances of finding true love? I'll put on an extra layer of SPF 100 and hope for the best.

```
Sounds like fun! When do you want to go?
Lucas: Are you free tomorrow?
Me: Yeah, I am,
```

Shit. Lying is not how you should start any relationship, even if it is just a friendship. But I can't ruin my slim chances by telling him immediately that I can't be in the sun. I don't want to scare him off before I get to know him. I *could* scare him off afterward, if need be, like the time Rosie set me up with a blind date with one of James' colleagues from work.

She told me that we had loads in common and he seemed like a great catch. He was a tall, lanky man, with premature hair loss. He walked as if his head was too heavy for his shoulders and he spoke with a rasp. The smell of stale tobacco wafted in the air as he sat down in the chair opposite mine. The restaurant was poorly-lit, and the seating areas were huddled together, not facilitating personal space.

As each course arrived, the size of yoyos, getting smaller and smaller, he told me that he was an avid reader of erotica, his eyes lighting up as he said it, as if images of the said erotica lit up his brain as soon as the words left his mouth. For the entire dinner, he went on about his admiration for authors of the genre. To be fair, Rosie did mention that she hadn't met the guy before, but according to James, he's delightful.

After our meal, he leaned over and whispered, "Are you into bondage?" His eyes twinkled.

I jerked back and decided to play along. "Of course, but I haven't really been into it since I crippled my last lover…" I bit my lip, my voice slow and husky, hoping the idea would repulse him.

His eyes lit up once again. He was on the edge of his seat. He covered my hand with his large hairy hands and shifted closer. The strong smell of tobacco on his breath now made the small amount of food in my stomach churn furiously. "Let me take you home, I want to show you my—"

I put my hand up and stopped him from speaking. My plan had backfired. I desperately searched for more ways to get out of the date, then I blurted out, "I'm allergic to the sun."

The fire in his eyes barely flickered. "Oh, that's no problem, we will be indoors." He winked.

With the food hanging out at the bottom of my throat, I continued, "Yeah, but a little bit of sunlight and my skin…it becomes scaly… and it itches…a lot, and I get red scaly bumps that sometimes fill with pus." I could see the fire die out as I explained, in the most detailed way possible, what would happen even with a minimal amount of exposure.

Sure, I exaggerated a bit.

I pushed my chair back and got up to leave. "I have to leave now, but please call me," I pleaded, pushing forward a folded napkin, with my actual number in it, toward his stunned face.

To this day I still don't want to imagine what he wanted to show me, and of course, I haven't heard from him, but if there is one thing I learned from this entire experience, it's that James needs to revisit the definition of 'delightful'.

So, it looks like I'll be going jet-skiing tomorrow.

I look down at the reply. Let's meet at 7.

I send a thumbs up and put my phone down. I squeeze my face into my pillow. I know I'll regret this.

Chapter 7

My alarm rings the next morning. I get up instantly. The thought that I'll be jet skiing today with a hot guy— and then burned to a crisp in the sun—proves to be an effective alarm. I chuckle over my 'hot' pun, as I gulp down some water.

I run a quick shower and pull on my most conservative piece of swimwear. I blend a smoothie and sip it while I thought of how to get around my problem. Unless there exists a portion of the ocean that is shaded (why isn't there such a thing?), I am stuck.

This is why they say that honesty is the best policy, but they're not too clear on when exactly it would be best. They should really lay down the rules more clearly, exceptions included, to this policy.

Exceptions:

1. When you're trying to make a good first impression on your very hot neighbour.
2. When you are trying to convince your best friend that her ex just broke up with her because he actually likes her too much, and will soon realise his mistake.
3. When your mom asks you if your aunt's *koeksisters* are better than hers, and you want to spare her feelings.

Smoothie cup drained, I rub sunscreen lotion all over my body and face, twice. I slip on my flip-flops, grab a towel and bag with all my essentials, and hurry out the door.

Downstairs, Lucas is already waiting— in board shorts—and OMG, he is freaking shirtless! I guess perfection does exist after all.

"Morning," he says, studying me from head to toe, perhaps in relief that I'm not wearing a hazmat suit.

"Morning," I reply with a smile, dragging my eyes from his chiselled physique.

The water-sports shed is less than a hundred-metre walk from the apartment entrance. But I shield my face from the glare of the walkway just in case. Outside the shed, a pile of kayaks is piled on top of one another, while rows of oars leaning against its wall. About fifty metres away, jet skis are tied to a small wooden jetty.

I catch myself trying to scratch my skin. We shouldn't be that long, right? A quick ride across the water and back into the safety of the shade.

"Morning Rahul, two jet skis, please," Lucas' silky voice cut into my thoughts. He's talking to the assistant at the shed.

"Err, Lucas…" I say, feeling the heat build in my cheeks.

He turns his head to look at me, a quizzical expression on his face.

"I haven't ridden one before… Err… I don't know…"

Lucas nods. He seems cool about it and turns back to the assistant.

"We'll just take one— to share."

I try waving my card at Rahul to pay, but Lucas brushes it off, and hands over cash.

We follow Rahul to the rickety jetty. Lucas hands me a life-jacket as Rahul unties one of the machines.

We thank Rahul, and he wanders back to his post.

Lucas climbs on and reaches his hand out to take mine. My hand feels small in his as he pulls me up behind him. "You will have to hold me, OK?"

"Sure," I reply.

I try to wrap my arms around his jacket but I can't get a good grip.

"That's not going to work, you'll fly off. I hope I don't get into trouble for this," he says, taking off his life jacket, and throwing it onto the jetty. "You should be fine now," he continues.

"Uhm… why?" I ask hesitantly.

"You can hold me properly now," he says, running his fingers through his wavy hair.

Holy shit. "Like put my hands on your body?" I ask cautiously.

"Yes, Diana. Unless you prefer falling off," he says, laughing.

"Are you sure you're comfortable with that?" I ask nervously not wanting to be too forward.

"I'm fine, Diana. Relax," he replies.

I wrap my arms around his warm body, gently trying to make as little contact as possible. At that point, I don't think I'm actually touching him, but as soon as he starts the engine, the jet ski lurches forward. My fingers sink into his skin, as if my life depends on it, my face smashing against his back at first. I lift my face up once he steadies, and apologise. The wind blows through my hair while we hop across the ocean.

I feel liberated. The air is filling my lungs and the sun is shining on my face. I hardly ever get to enjoy the sun. As if sensing my freedom, my body starts heating up from the inside. The millions of tiny ants start crawling all over again. The sting of the salty water isn't making it any better. I watch my skin begin to flush slightly on my thighs and arms. I try to enjoy the ride, but man, my skin is starting to tingle and burn. I am so focused on mentally driving the ants away, so I don't squirm behind Lucas, making him think I'm making a move on him, that I don't realise when we eventually slow down and make our way back to shallow water, toward the jetty. Rahul is waiting for us with Lucas' lifejacket in his hand, and he looks relieved when we pull up.

I jump off hurriedly.

"So what did you think?" Lucas asks, his smile wide and his eyes bright.

" It was splendid Lucas, thanks," I say flatly, trying to keep the discomfort and jumping down to a bare minimum.

"We should do it again sometime," he says, looking at me sceptically.

I nod vigorously. "We should. Yeah."

Noticing my jumpiness, he asks, "Are you all right? Do you feel a bit sick? It's normal for the first time but you will settle down soon. We can wait a bit before we grab a coffee."

"Yeah…. you know what, my tummy isn't feeling great. I'm just gonna head back home," I say, hating the words coming out of my mouth. I back away, waving. "Thank you so much, Lucas. I had fun."

He smiles weakly, obviously trying to work out what is going on.

I trudge back to my apartment, pushing the door open. I glance at my reflection in the mirror. My neck, chest, and shoulders are covered in red blotchy patches. My hands have begun to swell and my thighs have fine white bumps all over the red skin. I gulp down a few antihistamine tablets and take a shower.

I have ruined our first outing together. I have not thought the jet-skiing through. At all.

****

The next morning, I jump out of bed. The ants have finally surrendered, and clear thoughts enter my mind again. I place a few croissants in a basket, cut up some slices of cheese, and wash a bowl of grapes. I French-press some coffee and arrange it all on a big tray with crockery and cutlery. The tray is too full to carry out with me and ring his door-bell at the same time, so I leave it on the kitchen counter and go to Lucas's front door. I ring the bell and step back. I wait a few moments, then the door opens. Lucas is standing in pyjama pants and is wearing a T-shirt, thank God.

"Do you mind holding the door open for me?" I ask.

Not waiting for a reply, I walk over to my apartment and bring the tray back with me. I walk straight inside, leaving the tray on the table.

"How did you know I was home?" he asks.

"I didn't," I wink.

I study his apartment, taking everything in. It's exactly like mine yet, somehow, quite the opposite. It's warm and inviting. Where are the surfboards along the walls, heaps of wet towels and dishes piled on every flat surface? Instead, his plants are alive, and magazines are neatly stacked on his coffee table. I scan his TV cabinet, which is arranged with framed photos and ornamental elephants.

"Do you get a maid in here?" The words spill out of my mouth.

He laughs, clearly noticing the shock in my voice. "No, actually. I like cleaning," he says.

I look around again and mouth the word 'wow.'

"This is an apology breakfast," I say, gesturing to the tray.

"I accept," Lucas says, picking up a grape and popping it into his mouth. "So what happened?" He asks as he sits down.

I join him at the table. "I went for a desert safari the night before last, and I think I ate something that didn't agree with me," I reply calmly. I rehearsed that bit while preparing the breakfast. "I'm feeling much better now," I add.

We make our way through the fruit, croissants, and coffee. When I mention that I'm from South Africa, he tells me that he'd been there before. He is from New Zealand. We troll each other about each other's national rugby team.

"So, Lucas, what do you do?"

"I am a diving instructor,"

"Oh…sounds exciting," I say.

"It is, just being out in the deep vast ocean gives me a rush. I love anything that can give me that rush. It makes me feel alive." His eyes sparkle as he speaks. "The freedom when you just jump out of a plane or drop from a cliff into the waves." He smiles, wary of me watching him. "It's… you know…"

No, I don't, all the activities he's just mentioned sound like death-wishes to me.

"It makes me feel invincible." He continues. I can keep an open mind, but just hearing about it makes my stomach knot up.

We get up from the table and I ask him about all the little bits and pieces on his TV cabinet. He walks me through skiing in Switzerland, base camp at Kilimanjaro, and white-water rafting in Tsitsikamma National Park (been there, looked at the people doing it, got a panic attack, walked in the opposite direction) and his most recent adventure—skydiving over the Palm Jumeirah.

"No books?" I ask him.

"Nah, not for me. Just sitting in one place, holding a book for hours…. I can't think of anything more boring." He shivers as if the idea actually haunts him at night.

The statement hits me like a punch to the stomach. Still absorbing the shock, I manage a smile. I'm being immature. He doesn't *read*…he doesn't read *books* or *like* reading books. It's no reason he would not like me. Am I in high school? Where superficial similarities make or break a relationship? We are both mature adults who don't need to have every single thing in common to make a relationship work. I am *not* insecure.

I am *very* insecure.

"So what do you do?" he asks, distracting me from my pep talk.

Do I lie? No, I'm already lying about too many things. This is not good. Just tell him. Nothing bad is going to happen. I gulp. "I'm an—"

My phone rings in my bag. It's a call from Theo. He's saved the day. "I have to take this, give me five minutes?" Lucas leads me into his room.

"Hey Theo, what's up?" I ask casually. Not really listening to Theo on the other end, I let my eyes wander around Lucas's room.

The large bed is covered in beige bedding, and the rug in front is minimal yet comfortable and warm. A sturdy-looking headboard, oak closets on either side of a door that probably leads into a bathroom, like mine.

"Diana? Hello? Are you there?" I jerk back to my phone call. "Sorry, I'm here, please go on," I say, feeling guilty for not paying attention. Yes, bad manners and unprofessional. I couldn't help myself.

"Have you recovered from the other night?" he repeats, I'm sure.

"Yeah, mostly, and you?"

"'I'm OK. It was fun."

"Even the vomiting?" I joke.

Theo laughs. "I just edited that part out. Speaking of editing, I was hoping you could send me a few more chapters. I don't mind making some headway."

"Sure, no problem, I will forward them in an hour."

"Great. Bye." With that, he hangs up.

I go back into the dining room and see that Lucas is out on the balcony watering some of his plants. I step outside into the warm air.

"I have to go," I say, frowning and pouting my lips. Relief washes all over me. I can postpone this discussion till another day. "Can we pick this up later? I have to work."

"Sure," Lucas says, following me back into the living room. I pile up the dishes on the tray, and fumble for my bag. He hands the tray to me, placing his large warm hand over mine as I take it from him, and says "I am having a housewarming party on Friday. Please come?"

"It will be small, low-key, just very chilled," he adds.

"I'd love to," I reply with a smile. Back in my apartment, I scan my living room as I empty the contents of the breakfast tray. Butterflies dance around in my tummy as I recall the moment he invited me to his 'small, low-key' housewarming party. He thinks I'm special enough to be included in his little circle. I feel the warmth rise up to my cheeks.

Step one of the plan— get to know his interests—was completed. And it had been pretty easy.

I open Instagram and search for him in the name of more research on Step One. His profile is private. I bite my lip, clicking on follow. He accepts instantly and sends me a friend request as well, which I accept instantly too.

I scroll through his profile, being careful not to double-tap any pictures. There isn't much. There are a few pictures of him with some horses, either riding, grooming, or holding them. A few with a group of people kayaking in mangroves. That's about it. I'll need to work on step two a bit harder: hanging out at the places that he did. That's going to be a tough one. It seems like he only hangs out in the sun.

I snap out of it, remembering that Theo is expecting some of my work. He's working on a specific timeline so that I can submit my best work for the festival. Though, I'm not entirely certain why he's under so much stress. Rosie will be back by then. I guess he's trying to make a good impression on the company.

I sit down at my laptop and open it. A WhatsApp message pops up. Rosie is inviting me to a Zoom meeting. Once I join, I immediately see Rosie's beautiful face. Hair all over the place, her bright hazel eyes in her thinner face exaggerating, her dark circles. She connects to audio a few seconds later.

"Motherhood has been kind to you," I joke, "but I need you back at work."

"Oh tell me about it," she chimes in. "The best part is all the weight I've lost breastfeeding." She pauses and then continues, "and the baby of course." We both giggle.

"So, why are you in such a good mood?" she asks. "I haven't seen a smile this wide on your face since…" She broke off, tapping her fingers to her chin, "Since Hilary—"

"Don't say her name!" I interrupt.

I take a deep breath and my wide smile resumes. "Rosie," I say calmly, "Of course, I've smiled like this before, all the time—" I throw my hands in the air for dramatic flair.

Rosie cut me off. "It's a boy!" she exclaims.

"What? Are we twelve?" I reply, rolling my eyes.

She scans my face and gasps, "It *is* a boy! Tell me everything. No, wait, I want to hear it directly from you. Can you come over tomorrow?" she asks, her eyes wide.

"Absolutely," I say. "Give my love and kisses to Sonia and my best to James. I've got to get cracking on some work." I blow a kiss to her.

Rosie's face stiffens for a second and then she ends the meeting. What is that about?

I open up my documents, scan through the chapters I'm sending to Theo, and make a few edits here and there before forwarding it to him. I hope I impress him.

Chapter 8

Theo and I settle in our seats across from each other at Forever Coffee, a minimalist-styled café on the Yas Bay waterfront. A slight breeze moves through the air, carrying away any humidity. A waitress comes over, scribbles down our orders, and heads back to the kitchen.

Theo pulls out a stack of paper from his bag and lays them on the table. He pushes them forward.

"These are edited. There are very few changes."

I flip through each page. Next to each paragraph where the edits usually are, I notice little drawings of the scenes. It's like watching a cartoon version of my chapter. "You brought my stories to life," I muse. "Consider me impressed."

"I hope you don't mind?"

"Not at all, I mean it was crap, yeah I would have," I look up at his startled expression, then quickly add, "but these are great. Wow."

Theo mocks relief and chuckles. "Good to know,"

"If I don't win this competition, I could turn my stories turn it into an animated TV series," I tease.

"Always good to have a plan B."

I tuck the stack of paper into my bag as the waiter places our coffees on the table.

"So how did you get into drawing?" I ask, wanting to unpack more.

"My grandfather actually. When I was five or six, he bought me an entire case of pencils for my birthday… you know those tin cases?"

I nod.

"And I just wanted to impress him, so every afternoon, after school, my grandfather would pick me up, and while I waited for my mom to fetch me, I would take out my pencils and begin working on something and he would join me…it became our thing…and he would teach me all the different drawing techniques… and he would draw pictures for me to colour in…" he trails off.

I sip my coffee. "That is beautiful, and he taught you well." My words bring Theo back to the present.

"My mother doesn't approve of my making a career out of it." His voice is low and steady.

"Why not?"

"She believes I should have a *real* job."

"A real job?" I lift my eyebrows.

"Yes. A teacher, a lawyer—…"

"—or a doctor," I say, finishing his sentence.

He lets out a single breath, the corner of his mouth curving. "Your parents too huh?"

"Not mine, but Rosie's. Her mother fainted when she told them that she had dropped out of med school."

Theo's eyes widened. "Wow."

"Yeah…But for me, it was different. Writing was a way for me to escape my allergy…I used to have panic attacks every time we needed to leave the house, and my mom got me into therapy… and the psychologist recommended keeping a journal…and after a while of writing what went through my mind every time I thought about being in the sun I just decided to write stories about myself in a world where I didn't have this allergy… and now…I'm here…many moons later. And I guess my parents just went with it."

"So that's how you started writing."

"Yeah." I caution a smile, not entirely sure why I had dug out some of the most painful moments for Theo. "Are you disappointed that it wasn't one of those moments where I picked up a pen and the air began glowing around me, and I suddenly knew I'm meant to write stories for the rest of my life?"

"Kind of. Yes." He says, deadpan.

I grin and sip my coffee.

"Is drawing a passion of yours?"

"Yeah, it definitely is, I put myself up on Fiverr, as an illustrator, and I've been landing a few jobs. I'm hoping to build up a portfolio so companies can see my actual talent. I have a few illustrations, but some companies don't take them seriously if someone hasn't used my work in their branding or product."

"So why doesn't your mom approve?"

"Well…" Theo shifts in his seat.

"You don't have to tell me; I know it's personal," I say quickly, suddenly regretting digging a bit too deep.

"It's not that, I'm trying to figure out a way to tell you why, without painting her as the parent who 'doesn't support her child's dreams.' That's the first impression many people have about her."

"I understand…" I say, unsure if he wants to continue the conversation.

"Yeah. Well, anyway, she's a single mom with no financial help from my father. And when we were growing up, she had to take jobs that she didn't particularly enjoy, but they paid well. And it's not that she doesn't get my passion or doesn't want me to be happy. She's just not sure that my passion can bring in money… and money is always a touchy subject for her."

Theo leans back in his chair and looks up. Then he leans forward, the creases around his eyes relaxing. He brings his hand an inch closer to mine. My eyes dart to his hand very near to mine and I can feel the slightest tingle of awareness.

His eyes fixate on mine for a moment too long. I clear my throat, pulling my gaze away from him, and sip from my empty cup. Dammit.

"I see the way you work. That joy, that emotion. I feel it in your writing too. I feel it when I'm drawing. Brings back the best memories too." His smokey eyes flash a shade of blue. His fingertips brush against mine. The tingle grows into a full-on shock wave through my hand. What the hell is with the static in this humid place?

Chapter 9

The next morning, the Uber crunches over the gravel outside Rosie's villa. I get out of the car, a gift for Sonia and a bouquet of Rosie's favourite flowers, peonies, in my hands. I thank the driver and he leaves. I walk up to the gate and pressed the intercom. I'm immediately buzzed in.

Rosie stands at the front door with her arms opened wide. She grabs hold of me and plants a kiss on each of my cheeks. As I enter, she takes the things from my hands and leads me to the dining room. She leaves Sonia's gift at the base of the stairs and immediately unwraps the peonies to get them in a vase filled with fresh water. All the while, she updates me on all the details of her labour and delivery and her lack of sleep. Then she tells me that Sonia is having her nap, and gives me a detailed walk through their daily routine.

"How's it going with Theo?" she asks. "Is he any good? Are you comfortable working with him?"

"So far, I have no complaints. He seems thorough."

"Are you sure? We can always get someone else, it's not too late—"

"He's great. Really. He lent me his pyjamas that day we first met," I giggle. Rosie picked up the glee in my voice. She lifted her eyebrows.

"What?" I ask.

"OK, he's a gentleman. Is he a good editor? Do you like working with him?" she asked.

"I just said that I did."

"I'm just double-checking that he is actually good at the job he's employed for."

"What is that supposed to mean?"

"He cooked for you? You went on a desert safari? He lent you his pyjamas? What's next? A romantic hot air balloon ride? He's your editor, Diana. Not the next eligible bachelor," she says, sounding annoyed.

"You're overreacting. Yeah, we did a few things together but it was completely platonic. Unorthodox I admit, but he's never been to Abu Dhabi and I'm just showing him around. Being friendly. And we've been working too. Besides he's got a girlfriend."

Rosie looks at me apprehensively, picking up the disappointment in my voice.

"Not that it matters because he's my editor," I say quickly. "And I met someone!"

"Oh yes! You did!" Rosie squeezes me. "I'm sorry for the interrogation. I'm just looking out for you."

"I appreciate that," I say weakly, rubbing my sore ribs.

"Now tell me about this guy you met?" she demands inquisitively.

"Well, he's my neighbour…"

"Oooh. That's convenient."

I relay the jet-skiing and the make-up breakfast, the invite to the party, and my plan to try and 'bump' into him when he goes horse-riding.

Rosie raises her eyebrows again. "Sounds like hard work."

"No, I'm just taking the opportunity to try new things, be adventurous," I say, trying to convince myself, I mean, Rosie.

"You hate adventure and new things. You watch the same shows and read the same books because you already know what's going to happen."

"Exactly. And that's probably why I'm still single," I retort.

She sighs in surrender. "As long as you're happy."

"I am," I say, jutting my chin out in defiance.

We sit in silence for a while, sipping our juices. It's awkward. Things are hardly ever awkward between Rosie and me. Something must be wrong. I lift my head and open my mouth to ask and then Rosie speaks in a quiet and steady tone.

"Diana." She takes a deep breath. "I've resigned from AT."

I stare at her, blankly. I want to scream but instead, I try to keep calm. I probably should have attended a few more of Caitlyn's meditation classes.

"Are you OK?"

"Why didn't you tell me earlier?"

"I didn't know that I wanted to resign until I held Sonia in my arms. I always thought I would take a few extra months of leave, then juggle work and motherhood. But I can't imagine leaving Sonia now…"

Tears glisten in her eyes. Watching her, my eyes begin to well up.

"Of course, I understand, yeah, I am taken a bit off-guard, but we will make it work," I say, hugging my best friend. "I'm proud of you for making this tough decision."

"And I'm proud of you for agreeing to go out with someone after all these years," she jokes. "Even if you are trying to kill yourself in the process."

I roll my eyes.

"I'm still your friend. And we can talk about your work whenever you want. I just can't handle the pressure to meet deadlines now."

I rub Rosie's arm. "I understand Rosie. Don't worry about it." I smile. I will most certainly worry about it enough for both of us.

Chapter 10

Friday has finally arrived. Although I have a mild case of the jitters, I have to quickly recover before I meet my family for lunch. Fridays are family days in the Dawson household. Even though the UAE has changed to a Saturday-Sunday weekend from a Friday-Saturday one, family Fridays remain. My brother and I help my mother prepare lunch, or if the weather is good we have a *braai* in the backyard. Considering we are still in mid-summer, it's just lunch indoors with the air-conditioning set to 24 degrees C.

My parents are quite fond of Middle Eastern cuisine, so my mother tries her hand at making her own *zaatar manakish* and hummus. I prepare the *fattoush* and my brother sets the table. My father's job is to make fresh mint lemonade, filled with ice, and vibrant mint leaves. Having lived here for so long our palettes are accustomed to the various cuisines the country offers. Once we gather around the table and fill our plates, we each take a turn to relay the week's events.

I update them on Rosie resigning, some of Sonia's new milestones, and an incident at AT that involved Kate, my manager, enforcing a 'no body parts in the fryer rule.' It's good to know we have a fryer, but I don't think I'll be using it, ever, even if she were referring to the body parts of a chicken. And Theo, which brings a swirl in my stomach. It's probably something I ate. My brother, Sam, tells us about new dishes they've added to their menu and him sadly missing bumping a sheik by minutes as he came in for dinner.

My mother has picked up new hobbies like yoga and pottery. She tries to keep away from screens after spending a lot of her working life in front of them, as a high school computer studies teacher. My father, on the other hand, reminds me of teenagers who have to be pulled away from screens. He even has an Instagram account. His only follower is his sister, who is two years older than him.

I deliberately don't tell them about Lucas right now, even though I will eventually. Any time I mention a boy, my father just grunts and pretends that he didn't hear the conversation at all. My mother starts planning my wedding and picking out names for my future children. Or she goes into full panic mode about whether he is the one who would be able to accept my allergy. My brother goes through it as well. I specifically remember my brother bringing home a girl—the chef school equivalent of a lab partner—for a project, and my mother walked in casually, chatted to the girl about who knows what, and then asked her what she thought about the name Daniel for a boy. I've never seen the girl again, but I'm pretty sure my brother mentioned that she'd moved back to Portugal four weeks later. Coincidence? I think not.

After we clear up, I tell my mum that I won't be staying for dinner. So she packs some leftovers for me and gives me strict instructions on how to reheat them. My parents could be a bit overkill sometimes, but I believe I'll only understand why 'when I have kids of my own.' Once she'd double-checks that the cooler bag has everything I'll need for the night, she continues filling me in on the techniques she's been learning in pottery class.

Once I'm home, I store everything away in the fridge. I smell my clothing. Zaatar. That is not a good scent on a human being so a shower it has to be.

Once I'm sure that I smell like coconut (according to the body-wash bottle) I change into my most casual slash sexy but not too sexy but kind of hot floral wrap dress and pull a brush through my hair.

I walk over to Lucas's with the cheeseboard I had arranged (and re-arranged). I smooth down my dress and pat my hair once again. Lucas opens the door for me. I should be taken with his rugged face and welcoming smile but instead, I immediately focus on about twenty people crammed into his apartment. All chatting, drinks in hand, and all dressed rather casually. I can't tell if there's any music on or if the chatter of twenty people together miraculously has a rhythm.

Low key?

I leave my cheeseboard at the edge of the table, equally as out of place as I am, among the bowls of popcorn, crisps, and mini-chocolate bars.

As if reading my mind, Lucas says, "It got out of hand, I'm sorry."

I swallow the dryness in my mouth and force a smile. "Introduce me."

He takes me by the hand and leads me to the living room. He introduces me to his friend, a tall athletic blonde called Kevin, a colleague from work. Then there's Anita from the UK, her shiny brown hair convincing me she could be in a shampoo commercial. Next to her, Sandy. She has platinum blonde hair bobbed below the ear and an intricate floral tattoo running up her arm all the way to her ear. She also works at the diving school. And then there's Sanjay, a 'college friend.' His eyelashes put us ladies to shame and his hair is perfectly coiffed.

I shake hands with each of them.

"Who are all the others?" I ask Lucas, gesturing around the room.

"Friends of friends. They heard the word 'party'," he laughs.

Just then the bell rings, and Lucas leaves to open the door. Sandy tells me to sit and get comfortable, but after looking around the room, I realise there isn't any free space to sit.

"Thanks," I say awkwardly, and just move out toward the edge.

A tall lady, with hair in long curls down her shoulders, strides in. She's wearing washed-out jeans and a white linen tank top with lace detail, and black flip-flops. Wow. I want to be her when I grow up. Her face rings bells in my mind. Lucas and she chat effortlessly as she leaves a bottle of wine on the crowded table.

He brings her to the living area where his actual friends are sitting and chatting among themselves. They all greet her by name and she hugs each one.

Then Lucas brings her over to me. "Diana, this is Alison; she heads our kayaking group."

No wonder her face looks familiar, I have seen her on Lucas's Instagram account.

"Hi," I say, putting my hand out, "nice to meet you."

"Hello, love, nice to meet you! You're the neighbour, right? Lucas told me," she says in the clearest, most crisp British accent I've heard.

"Oh?" I look over at Lucas, hoping he doesn't notice that the shape of my irises have probably changed into hearts. He spoke about *me* to someone else? Butterflies float around in my stomach.

"Yeah," he says casually. "I told her I found one more person for our kayaking group." He looks at me, raising his eyebrows. Who is the extra person they're inviting to their group? I turn my head around me. Alison and Lucas are still watching me, waiting for me to speak. Oh! "Me?" My voice comes out louder than I expect.

I have no idea why he has the impression that I'll be keen to join his kayaking group, but I decide to just go with it considering step three of the plan (get to know his friends) seems to be working itself out.

I nod. "Yeah. I've been looking for a group to join actually. Kayaking on your own sucks. Especially if you get stuck, you know." According to a book

I've read. It'll also be the perfect opportunity to spend more time with Lucas and get to know him better.

Alison laughs. "Exactly," she says. "So let's share digits." She pulls out her phone. We exchanged 'digits' and I'm instantly added to the group called 'Mangrove Mayhem.'

"So who else is in the group?" I ask.

"All of them," she says, pointing to the whole lot of Lucas's friends whom I have already met. "And him." She points to a short little guy who reminded me of Lego figurines. "He's Jason, also new to our group."

"We go every Sunday morning, at six, in the summer. Is that OK for you?"

"Yeah, absolutely," I say trying to sound enthusiastic.

"Updates are posted on the group about timings and weather. Just bring your water bottle, cap, and plenty of sunscreen."

I bite my lip. "Of course,"

"But reminders are posted every week," Alison continues. She really takes this kayaking group seriously. She walks away and squeezes herself between Anita and Sandy on the couch. The magazines on the coffee table I'd seen earlier that week had been replaced by a card game.

Not able to find a seat, anywhere, I wander around aimlessly, nibbling on the cheese I'd brought, searching for Lucas as discreetly as I can. He's nowhere to be found. I'm not going to initiate any type of conversation because that means putting myself out there and opening myself up to rejection. I check the time on my phone. It's only been an hour. I lean back against a wall, now nibbling on my hair, waiting for Lucas to emerge.

A few moments later, he appears from the balcony. I shuffle over to him, manoeuvring my way through all the people in the room. "I'm gonna head off now," I say.

"Already?" he tilts his head.

"Yeah, it was a long day."

"I hope you had fun."

"Yeah, I did," I lie. "Thank you for inviting me."

He smiles and leads me out of the apartment. "I'll see you soon I guess," he says waving, as he closes the door.

I take a deep breath of air, which seems so much fresher than it is in there.

I kayak now, I'm learning new things about myself every day.

Chapter 11

On Sunday morning I'm back in my most conservative swimsuit and, having learned my lesson the last time I was out in direct sunlight, I take my antihistamines before the outing, still double-layering the SPF.

I put on a cap as well and make my way down to the watersports shed, the same place where we hired jet-skis from. The whole group is already all kitted out in their life jackets, fiddling with their oars as the guy from the shed, John pulls out each kayak.

My priority is to make sure I get paired up with Lucas. John hands me an oar. It's slightly lighter than I expect, thankfully. I push air with the oars trying to find a comfortable motion. No one seems to notice, much to my relief, but I have no way of knowing if I'm doing it correctly or not.

Once each person has their oar, we march as a group to the shore. There are four kayaks, three double-seaters, and one single-seater. Everyone effortlessly divides into groups. I make my way to get in the same kayak behind Lucas, but Jason, a small man as he is, shoves me out of the way and climbs in first. Not noticing, Alison got in behind Sandy. Great, I'm on my own. I put my first leg in and wobble about, finally getting my second leg in when I find my balance.

Alison turns around and shows me a thumbs up, which I return in kind. We all move swiftly from the shore and glide on the water toward the mangroves. At first, it seems easy to manoeuvre my kayak through the mangroves, but then we all take turns moving through the narrow alleys. The alley can fit two boats, so Kevin and Alison's boat go through first. I go in as well, but Lucas catches up with me.

"Having fun?" he asks.

"Yeah, I actually am," I say. It's true. Kayaking seems a lot easier and taking antihistamines early is keeping the tiny ants at bay, for now. I smile at him, admiring the way his locks turn into strands of gold. A sudden jerk startles me.

Oh, great! My kayak and oar are stuck somewhere in the mangrove plant. Pushing and pulling my oar in and out of the water to get it free, I knock Jason on the back of his head.

"Oww!" he screeches, and then growls, looking at me, eyebrows crunched.

I can't say he doesn't deserve it. He'd shoved me so he could get a seat with Lucas and left me all alone! I glare at him, "I'm *so* sorry Jake," I say insincerely.

"It's *Jason*." He narrows his eyes at me.

"I know." I shoot him a fake smile before he glides away from my sight.

Lucas and the rest of the group make some headway while I continue to struggle in the mangroves. I finally get free and make my way to them, but I'm a good few meters behind. They've stopped, and are now chatting and taking in the scenery while they wait for me.

It is a lovely day. I let the sun gently heat up my face as a slight breeze lazily rustles the mangroves. It's a feeling I'm not used to. The water is calm and our kayaks rock from side to side. It's one of those moments in your basic everyday life when you take a breath, and show gratitude for the little things around you.

We head back to the shore and get off our boats. We each hand our oars to John, the shed guy, who rests them against the wall.

Immediately, two young men from inside the shed come out with bottles of disinfectant and cloths in their hands. They spray and wipe each kayak in sync before taking them back into the shed. Synchronised disinfecting could be an Olympic sport by the time the pandemic is over. I check my watch. It's still before nine.

Lucas steps forward toward me, his hair wet, and his sleeveless shirt hanging over his body, but not hiding the lines along his skin defining his arms and chest.

A single breath leaves my mouth. It is quite obvious that he has descended from Greek Gods. He runs his fingers through his hair, to move it back. "You have good aim," he says sarcastically.

"Excuse me?" I ask, confused.

"We all saw the knock you gave Jason on his head."

"Oh! Yikes. I kinda get the idea that he deserved it," I say, feeling guilty for judging the Lego man without actually knowing him.

"Oh yeah, he definitely did," Lucas replies. "But, he's actually a nice guy, just a bit needy."

We both look over to Jason appearing to be complaining quite animatedly to the model-legged Alison about the bump that I'd given him on his head. Lucas and I glance at each other from the corner of our eyes and snort laughter.

I walk over to Jason. "I'm really sorry, Jason."

He grunts and stomps away.

Lucas rests his eyes on me. I meet his gaze, looking into his brilliant blue eyes. "You seemed to have a good time." He gently brushes sand off my surprisingly tanned arm. My heart jolts.

"You were as white as a ghost when I first met you," he says, knitting his eyebrows. He gazes into my eyes, expecting to find the answers there. Now my stomach jolts.

I quickly look away, afraid of what he'd see the truth. "I don't really go out into the sun," I say.

He cocks his head. "Why not?" OK, well, he's asking. I'd as well be honest. "I'm—"

Alison interrupts, saving me from having to provide an explanation. I'm grateful but annoyed that she interrupted our *moment*. "Do you guys want to grab a bite?"

"Yes," we both reply. Alison turns around, her luscious locks swinging behind her, and we follow.

The group enters the small cafe at the end of the beach front. The waitress, Jenna, immediately leads us through the cosy room to our table. After we all settle down along the leather couches lining the eighties-themed wall, Jenna hands out the menus.

I sit down next to Lucas. Being so close to him, my heart jumps into my mouth, and my brain seems to whirl and twirl. I'm seeing words on the menu but not reading, hearing chatter, but not listening. My only sense is my extreme awareness of him right next to me, and my bare knee touching his warm thigh. I scan the menu, already knowing that I'll have my usual from this cafe—fried eggs with green chili toast, served with hash browns and sweet *karak* tea.

Lucas orders the same thing as I do. Apparently, we *do* have something in common. I don't pay attention to what the rest of the group orders. While we wait, I pick up new bits of information about Lucas's friends. Alison is a kindergarten teacher. Anita only moved to Abu Dhabi a year ago. Jason is from Australia and moved here for work. He's on a contract and can't wait to get back home. He reckons the desert doesn't agree with him. I guess he doesn't venture into the Australian Outback then. Sandy is from New Zealand, like Lucas. She has a hint of an accent, unlike Lucas, who speaks more clearly than any other Kiwi I've met as if he had been trained for Hollywood.

Lucas turns to me and asks, "So what do you do?"

Without hesitation, I say, "I'm an author."

I study his face. No disappointment, confusion, or despair. Just plain ol' acceptance. He nods his head. "That's cool." See Diana, you had nothing to worry about.

Anita squeals. "I knew you looked familiar! You're Diana Dawson. You wrote 'The Monster Inside Me'?"

"Yeah," I say, looking down at my palms, heat rising to my face.

"My nephews and nieces love it! They're waiting for the next one! Is there going to be another one? Are you allowed to tell?" Her face brightens with excitement.

"Let's just say I'm working on it."

She squeals again.

The other diners whip their heads in her direction. She doesn't seem to notice. We all chat about our families, our home countries, and the pros and cons of each of our jobs. Our food arrives and everyone goes silent, enjoying whatever is in front of them.

Step three is coming together without much effort. Rosie is crazy for thinking that I'm 'trying too hard.' If anything, the steps were following *me*, not the other way around.

It's just after ten when we end our breakfast. Lucas and I stroll back to the apartment slowly, in silence. Everyone else goes to their cars parked nearby.

As we near our doors, I say, "Well, this is me."

Lucas's eyes scan my face at me and his lips curl into a smile. "I had a good time," he says.

I turn to open my door, but Lucas grabs my arm. His gaze finds mine and he presses his lips into mine. I breathe his scent in deeply. It's spicy but fresh and there's a hint of the salty ocean. His lips are soft and move with mine.

When he pulls away, we're both breathing deeply. Keeping his hand on my neck, he bends down just enough so I can feel his breath on my neck and he whispers, "I've wanted to do that since the first time we met."

"In the hazmat suit?" My voice, slightly stuck in my throat, comes out husky.

"On the balcony," he says, his voice raspy and calm.

He crushes his lips onto mine again before eventually letting me go. After he goes into his apartment, I push my door open and close it behind me. As I replay the kiss in my head, butterflies dance around in my tummy.

Resisting the urge to text Lucas to tell him what a brilliant kisser he is, I text Theo instead. I imagine the happy, relieved look on his face when I tell him that he may be offered a permanent position because Rosie has resigned. They can offer it to him first. He texts back immediately setting a meeting for the next morning, suggesting coffee.

Chapter 12

We arrive at the cafe at the same time. Theo opens the door for me and follows me inside.

We make our way to the elevators, catching up on the weekend's events. His girlfriend was in town for a few days. I feel an unwelcome pang of envy. Completely ridiculous of course. I'm almost dating Lucas. I'm not exactly sure yet because we haven't spoken since yesterday.

We seat ourselves next to the window after we order at the counter. Iced coffee for me and an Americano for him.

"Is she still in town?" I ask casually.

"No, she flew back this morning. My room was so quiet this morning," he says with slight disappointment in his voice.

"What did you guys get up to?"

"She hadn't been to Abu Dhabi before, so we visited Yas Water World and Ferrari World, and we even went to Warner Brothers World." Is Theo dating a child? OK, OK, I'm being mean. I love Ferrari World myself, come on. I smile, tight-lipped while he continues. "We visited the mosque. The really big white one?"

"Sheikh Zayed Grand Mosque," I say calmly. At least make an effort to know the name.

He went on some more about his girlfriend. I cross my arms. I am slightly jealous and offended that it was not me who showed him all these wonderful attractions. I uncross my arms. I'm being irrational. But still, anger slowly builds up inside me. I don't know where it's coming from. Perhaps it's because Lucas ghosted me after our kiss. To be honest, I didn't think it was that bad. Why hasn't he texted or called? Why would he though? It was just a kiss. Not a marriage proposal.

"Rosie resigned!" I blurt out, cutting Theo off. I wait for the surprise on his face but there's none. He shifts in his seat, avoiding eye contact.

"I know," he says, looking at me cautiously.

I move back into my chair. "You know? How long have you known about this?"

"The job they offered me is permanent." He speaks calmly and waits for a reaction.

I feel as if I've taken a baseball bat to the face. A really stupid person who's taken a bat to the face. Realisation puts the pieces together like a puzzle. Rosie resigned before the baby, not after she was born, as she said. Why did she lie to me? I've spent enough time with Theo for him to tell me. Why did they both keep me in the dark for so long?

I am going to kill Rosie.

He places his cool hand on mine. A tingle moves along my hand. I'm immediately annoyed that my nerves reacted so quickly to his soft touch. I jerk my hand away.

"Are you OK?" he asks.

My throat tightens. "Why did you lie to me?"

"It wasn't my place to tell you. Rosie wanted to be the one to tell you. To be honest, I didn't know she would take this long."

"I see," I mutter, feeling a wave of betrayal and embarrassment wash over me. He makes sense. I understand. I still have a bone to pick with Rosie. I'm an adult, I can handle situations with maturity.

"So, will you have me as your new editor?" he asks, breaking the silence.

I roll my eyes as a smile works its way over my face. "As long as you're not lying to me about anything else. Work-wise."

"I promise," he says, and he smiles. I'm peering straight into his grey eyes that are ever so slightly tinted with blue. I peel my gaze away, turning my focus to the ice dissolving into my coffee.

We drain our coffees and plan to get my work submitted with a new timeline now that Theo will be helping me through the whole process for the festival.

Theo leans back in his chair. "We have our work cut out for us Dawson; I hope you're ready?" He lifts his eyebrow slightly and his mouth twists into a half smile. Damn, that half-smile.

"I won't take that question as an insult considering you don't know me for very long," I smirk. I slap my hands on the table and peer straight into his grey cashmere-shaded eyes, annoyingly warm and cosy. "I. Was. Born. Ready."

Keeping the smirk on his stupidly handsome face, he replies, "We'll see."

"Are you challenging me, Evans?"

"I want to see what Diana Dawson is really made of."

I fold my arms over my chest. "You're on."

"Thirty thousand words by week's end," Theo announces.

Easy. This guy is going down. "Or?"

"You're going to write a character based on me into your story."

My eyes widen and I gulp involuntarily. A *new* character. In my story. That I have already *planned*?

Theo observes me. "Scared?"

"And if I give you thirty thousand words by Friday?" My voice makes its way past the lump in my throat.

He strokes an invisible goatee on his chin. "I'll cook for you."

I scoff. "You're not getting off so easily Evans. But since I would love to try more of your food, I'll accept. Except, you will cook for me, Rosie and James. How's that?"

"Looks like I'll be having a quiet evening in on Friday. With take out."

He has no idea.

****

As soon as I'm home I dial Rosie. When she answers, the words pour out of my mouth, like an unstoppable train. "Rosie. Why didn't you tell me that you'd resigned sooner? Theo looked at me with pity! With pity! It was humiliating, you know, to be the last one to find out about this. What got into you? I thought we were going to talk about it together."

"I didn't want to freak you out. I'm—"

"Freak me out? Why would I freak out?" I yell, my voice strained and high-pitched.

"You're literally freaking out right now," she says flatly. She continues in a serene tone, like the one your massage therapist might use when asking you to relax and let go of any tension, "You were still busy finishing up your book. I didn't want it to be a distraction. And I wanted to see if Theo was a good fit." She's clearly rehearsed this moment.

"I felt like an idiot in front of Theo," I say a bit more calmly.

"You told me that if I left you'd never enter the competition. Would you have entered if I told you that I was resigning?"

74

"No," I say, "probably not. I'd rather you were honest with me though. I would have worked through it."

"I'm sorry, OK? I've found a good replacement for you, haven't I?"

I can't help but smile. I really do like Theo. There's just something about him that makes me feel at peace. His presence brings me peace. It just means that he's good at his job. He's able to soothe a highly-strung lion. Or cat.

The sound of Rosie's voice brings me back from my thoughts. "Don't overthink it, Diana. I love you. OK? Please believe me that I do things for your own good. As a friend and editor."

"Yah yah," I say, rolling my eyes. This is true. Rosie always looks out for me.

"By the way, you're having dinner at my place on Friday night. Theo's cooking."

Chapter 13

It's Wednesday. I've written roughly twenty-six thousand words already. I'm really looking forward to this meal. Even if Theo has no idea he's cooking yet. I must say, a good meal is a really great incentive to pump all these words out. It's as if Theo knows the way to a few good chapters is through my stomach.

Jamie and Isabella had come up with a plan to catch their stalker. They had found out it was their neighbour, Nate. He had accompanied them on their hike but faked his death. He was working with someone. But who?

I'm also very distracted by Lucas. Or rather, thoughts of Lucas. I haven't really seen him since last week. We have spoken, but there are no deep, meaningful conversations. Sure, I've been busy and I'm sure he's been busy too. According to him, you will be surprised at the number of people who want to learn to dive, so he has no end of clients.

It's been particularly difficult to get a move on with my work. My mind keeps flashing back to the moment he pulled me in and, without hesitation, kissed me. The butterflies perform a synchronised dance in my tummy again. I've forgotten what it's like to be newly dating. The rush. The kind of adrenaline I can get behind. Dating should be up there on the list of activities that give you the biggest adrenaline rush. Yes, there is such a list. And yes, I've checked. But are we dating?

Maybe he's just looking for something casual. Which I really won't mind either.

Actually, I do mind, I'm at the point in my life where I know that I'm ready for something more, something to go further and blossom into something that will last forever. But does being in a serious committed relationship require literal time like exercising or doing a grocery run? Of course, it does. That's a silly question. Time which I have less and less of because I am in full competition mode.

So, after this little self-exploration, I guess it's probably best to keep things casual.

I sit at my computer figuring out how Jamie and Isabella are going to trap Nate, so his accomplice would have to come and find him. This isn't the time to hit a slump. The ideas aren't not pouring out at the moment. I've been stuck in this glitch before.

I glance at my planning board again. There's the yellow post-it with the four steps to bumping into your crush. Having accomplished most of them I figured that there'd just be a sign on his head that says, "I am your boyfriend now because you have gone through all that trouble." I rip it off, squashing it in my hands before landing it in the bin.

Looking through the other notes on my board, I finally give up.

My doorbell rings. I've probably ordered something from somewhere that I've forgotten about. The woes of online shopping.

I pull on my gown and open the door. It's Lucas. His hair is wet, and a hint of clove wafts in through the door. He's wearing his usual black T-shirt and dark jeans. My favourite combination.

"Hey, do you have a moment?" His eyes light up, but the rest of his face gives nothing away.

"Err…I guess so?" I hesitate.

"Come on." He grabs my hand and pulls me out of the door. He doesn't seem to care that I'm in my pajamas and bunny slippers. What the hell is happening? Is someone in trouble? Gasping for air or dead already? Oh dear, perhaps it's the old lady from number 232. *Life is short, my child; learn to love*, she would always croak. I would ignore her, rolling my eyes, and now I feel guilty for being rude. Was she all alone when she died? So much for Caitlyn's 'special tea'. I wonder as I run with Lucas out of the apartment building. I expect to see a crowd around an ambulance, but it's just bright sunlight.

Sunlight!

Shit! I don't have any sunblock on. I stop walking and step backward into the shade.

"I can't go into the sun," I mumble.

Lucas cocks his head. "What?" He raises his eyebrows and smiles. "Oh, come on, it's just a few more steps and you will be in the shade, you don't need sunblock."

So, he reads minds. Totally OK with that. Not. Does he know that I'm allergic to the sun? Most importantly, how?

My eye catches the sight in front of me. I ignore the sun, and the ants coming out to play one by one. On a secluded spot on the beach, is a picnic blanket, underneath a fly-net lay a board of some sort of cheesy flatbread. There is a flask of something—judging by the shape, it was either *gahwa* or *karak chai*. There's a little pot of popcorn and a small bowl of chocolate-dipped strawberries beside it. And a bit of shade created by an umbrella. Lucas takes my hand in his and leads me to the sand.

"Surprise!" he says, his arms spread out.

I smile at him feeling guilty. How do I tell him I need to get my antihistamines ASAP? "You're crazy, you know that? I don't have proper clothes or my phone."

"Overrated," he says with a wink.

We sit down on the blanket, Lucas next to me. My body is on high alert, picking up on his slightest of movements.

He squints at me. I'm turning red; I can feel it.

"How did you know that I'm allergic to the sun?"

"Anita is always bugging me about wearing sunblock when I go out into the sun, and I figured it's a lady thing to worry about being in the sun without any of it." He pauses. "Wait, you're *allergic* to the sun?" His eyes widen.

"Yeah…I am…" I say, waiting for his reaction. This is the part where he asks if it's contagious. Silly, I know, allergies aren't contagious, but apparently, people lose their common sense when they're afraid of you.

Realisation sweeps over his face. "Explains a lot," he says. He cups my face in his large hand and places his lips on mine. He pulls back and says, "Wow, you're hot!"

"Oh, uhm," I stutter, not entirely sure whether it's a compliment.

He laughs, looking at my expression, "I mean your face is literally hot. Let's go inside."

"Of course, that's what you meant," I say, smiling. "Thank you," My heart is smiling too. He's not creeped out.

I begin packing everything up, but he puts his hand over mine. "You go, I will pack this up," he says, opening the cooler bag, and piling everything in.

"I'll meet you upstairs." I peck him on the cheek and dash upstairs.

I open my cabinet and pull out my antihistamines. Grabbing the bottle of water nearest to me I gulp them down. I hear shuffling outside, so I open the door. Lucas walks in with the cooler bag and picnic basket in his arms. He leaves everything on the table and begins studying my apartment.

I watch him carefully, his face revealing nothing. His eyes settle on my bookshelf. I feel myself wince.

"The house of a writer. Interesting," he says finally.

"Thank you," I say, still not quite able to make out how he really feels.

He turns to me with his eyebrows knitted, blue eyes darker than usual. "You know, it does worry me a little, that you're an author and you read so much."

There it is. I knew it. I thought that I was being insecure when he told me that he didn't like reading, I thought I was being immature. And I thought the sun would be the bigger problem. My heart begins sinking away. "Oh…" I croak; it's all I can manage.

He holds me by the shoulders and looks straight into my eyes. "You have weapons on your shelf!" His eyes brighten and he grins. He spins around again and gapes at the bookshelves brimmed with hardcovers.

I let out a heavy sigh, my heartbeat slowly steadying. "Well, you better be careful, I'm skilled in the art of book wielding."

"You have a unique talent, Miss Dawson," he jokes. He walks over to my dining table and begins laying out the food.

"Books aren't just for reading, you know," I smirk as I follow him.

He pulls out a chair and gestures for me to sit down. "Mademoiselle."

"Merci," I reply, sitting down. He pours *karak chai* into little cups, steam still swirling up into the air, filling it with the scent of cardamom. I bring the cup to my lips.

"So, you're allergic to the sun?" He narrows his eyes and searches my face.

"Yeah…" I say, looking down at the cup, and swirling the tea.

"So wouldn't kayaking and jet skiing be detrimental to your health?"

I laugh. "You invited me. Telling someone that I'm allergic to the sun the first time I meet them does not exactly leave the best first impression."

"Why not?"

"Well, I've had dates run away from me when I had a reaction…So I figured it's something I'd rather keep to myself for a while…"I trail off. I scan his face, which gives nothing away.

"So, what happens? What do you need to do to control it?"

"I need to wear SPF in direct sunlight. I can take antihistamines before I go out, but I try not to do that too often. I don't want my body to become too reliant on them, given I've got to take them in emergencies, for the rest of my life," I explain.

Lucas listens quietly, taking in everything I'm telling him. It feels good to finally be honest with him. I won't have to pretend around him anymore and he will completely understand.

"Anita said Sanjay was a friend from college?" I asked, hoping I'm not being too inquisitive. I gather our plates from the table and place them in the kitchen sink.

"Yeah, he is."

"Where did you study?" I ask, since he isn't exactly pouring out all the information at once.

"I studied at the University of Auckland." He stops there.

I become impatient. "OK… what did you study?"

"Accounting and finance," he says flatly.

I lift my eyebrows. "You're joking!" I say, unable to contain my disbelief.

"This is why I don't tell people about it. Underneath the boardshorts, they don't see a guy who just likes numbers."

I catch his eye. He pauses and we both burst out laughing.

"So you're a numbers guy?"

"Actually, I don't like numbers anymore, either. I don't want to spend the better years of my life in front of a screen."

"How did you get into diving?"

"I had some money saved up…and I found a niche for diving, so I opened the diving school."

"You own the diving school?" That's impressive.

"Yeah, I do, it's been a dream for a long time that's finally happening…I had all this money saved up and I wanted to do something I really enjoyed doing… and Alison suggested I do it here, and she already had a place for me to stay and needed some help with her mortgage."

"Alison?" My throat dries up. "I didn't know that you guys were so close,"

"Yeah, we're childhood friends. It's her apartment."

I guess he doesn't just live rent-free in my head.

He takes both my hands and spins me around, into his chest. I wrap my arms around his neck. He bends down and brushes his lips against my cheek, and then brings his lips to mine for a split second. He lifts his head up. Ugh. Diana wants more! I feel like pounding my fists on his hard chest.

"We are all going bowling tonight, do you want to join?"

"Yeah," I say, "that sounds like fun."

It isn't a total lie and it's not that I dislike Lucas's friends. It's just that I'd prefer to explore that kiss a bit more.

****

"I'm going to get some snacks," I yell over to Lucas, who is tying his shoelaces, over the sound of the blaring pop music. "What?" he yells back. I flap my hands at him, telling him not to bother. My stomach grumbles impatiently as I join the queue for nachos and milkshakes.

Tray in my hand, I make my way to the bowling lanes, most of which already have eager players huddled around. We team up, girls against boys. Lucas immediately begins explaining how to hold a bowling ball and the best way to knock down all the pins. I roll my eyes. Some men can't help themselves.

When it's my turn, I hurry over to Lucas. "Are my fingers in the right holes?" I ask. Yes, that came out terribly wrong. But I need to humour myself. He gives me a thumbs up. I turn around to face the lane and chuckle to myself.

I roll the ball down the lane, and it knocks all the pins down. The men roar with laughter around Lucas. After a few more scores, I notice Lucas's face turn pale, even in the dim lighting. I stick out my tongue, but his face stays rigid. "Lucas, you've never dated a girl who could beat you at anything," Sanjay jokes. Lucas's eyebrow twitches. It must be the lights.

The girls score tens as many times as Lucas's eyebrow twitches. He doesn't seem to be enjoying himself anymore. Not all people are dignified losers. I shrug it off and continue enjoying my winning streak.

I don't know what happened between this morning and the present, but who is this guy and where did he hide Lucas?

After bowling, the group decides to have dinner. Once we're seated around our table and the waitress takes our orders, the group discusses kayaking again this weekend.

"I don't think I'll join you guys this weekend," I say. My gaze meets Lucas's and there's understanding there. So I thought.

"Diana is actually allergic to the sun," he blurts out.

I choke on my orange juice and a bit of it goes up my nostrils.

I glare at Lucas. His mouth twitches as he glares back. What the fuck?

My gaze quickly shifts around the table. A few words and nods of sympathy, but thankfully no questions. I guess they just don't care about whether I'm there or not. I should be relieved. I smile weakly.

Why on earth did Lucas just share my condition with the others? I'd told him about it in confidence.

Think well of people, think well of people, think well of people. My heart is beating rapidly, and my breathing becomes shallower. Dammit. Once again, I find myself regretting not taking more of Caitlyn's meditation classes. I finally manage to control my breathing and I keep chanting my mantra for tonight. *Think well of people, I am going to kill him, think well of people think, how could he be such a dick? Think well of people, what a jerk!*

Once our food arrives, I try to push aside my thoughts and enjoy my cheeseburger. Mission failed. My mind is trying to work out what the hell just happened, like the cogs in a very rusty machine. What the *hell* had gotten into him? Why? But *why*? How could he be so insensitive? Will I never be able to confide in him? Is this the type of relationship I want?

There's only one way to have all (OK, not all, but some) of my questions answered. I have to *ask* him. Ugh, I hate confrontation. I bite through my burger, hoping each juicy, cheesy morsel that goes down will push away all the irritation building up in me.

I'll speak to him and everything will be OK. Every relationship should have its boundaries clearly marked out. It does not have to be a fight, or awkward. Just one adult telling another adult not to share secrets. Sounds ridiculous that I need to have this conversation with an adult. Maybe I need to make him a pinky promise.

After dinner, we leave the others, who make their way to their cars.

The evening is warm and peaceful except for the occasional hum of cars passing by. Lucas suggests we walk around a bit and spend time alone before we return home. Great, this will be the perfect opportunity to speak to him about how I feel.

He laces his fingers through mine. His hands are warm and slightly rough. We walk in silence for a few moments. I glance at him, enjoying the evening. OK, maybe I can forgive him a little for being insensitive. *Think good of people, think good of people, think good of people.*

Since he has nothing to say, I might as well bring up the secret telling and ruin the perfect moment. But I have to be honest with him. I felt embarrassed when he told his friends about my allergy. I glance at him again. There are shadows covering bits of his chiselled face, his hair falling carelessly on his neck.

"Luca—"

"Dian—"

He smiles and looks down, then turns to me.

"You go," I tell him. I can tell him my issue afterward.

"I had a really nice time tonight. I don't usually introduce my girlfriend to my friends so soon."

My heart does a little jig. He called me his girlfriend. My cheeks begin to heat up. And it isn't from the humidity. He swoops me into his arms and picks me up. Our lips lock. I fill my lungs with his scent. My fingers run through his hair. He puts me down and pulls away.

"You looked uncomfortable," he says, peering straight into my eyes.

Here we go. He needs to know. Just get it out of the way. "I was. Especially after you told all your friends that I'm allergic to the sun."

"Oh, uhm, I just wanted to be honest with them about why you couldn't join us."

"But it's not your place to tell them. I would have told them when I was ready."

"I'd have to lie to them about why you wouldn't be joining us on all our outdoor activities, and I didn't want them to think you were rejecting me," he argues.

Heat builds up in my chest. How many knocks to the head with an oxygen tank did this guy take?

"And they didn't even care, they didn't really say anything or like leave the table because the thought repulsed them," he persists, still trying to make his case.

"Exactly, Lucas, they don't care, so there was no need to tell them. And, I really do not think they'd think I'm rejecting you just because I can't attend one of your group activities. I have my own life."

I can't believe I'm having this conversation. Telling someone about my allergy has once again backfired. Not in the way I expected it to, I must admit.

He sighs heavily. "OK," he takes my shoulders looking straight into my eyes, "I'm sorry, OK, I was way out of line."

"Thank you," I say.

Then he lifts me up around my waist as if I'm nothing in his strong arms. He looks up at me. "I really am sorry."

Looking down at his face, my arms around his neck, I press my lips into his. "Apology accepted."

We call an Uber and jump in. Ten minutes later we're walking into our apartment building. I wave as he goes toward his apartment. I enter mine and close the door behind me, taking off my shoes, and leaving my bag and phone on the couch.

The warm spray of the water calms the dancing butterflies in my stomach. I think about the evening some more. There is a nagging feeling in my chest. But then he'd called me his girlfriend. And just the memory of that sent butterflies dancing again. And that kiss. Wow. Each one gets better than the one before.

****

It's Friday morning. I hit 'send' on a few chapters I've written with a total word count of thirty-two thousand three hundred and seventeen.

A text pops up on my screen:

```
Damn, Dawson. I better start planning dinner.
```

I tap a reply:

```
TBH, the new character that I hadn't written haunted
me into writing all those words. I told Rosie and James
that dinner is at 8
```

```
Theo: I'll be there at 6.30.  👍
```

At six twenty-five p.m. the doorbell rings.

"Hey." Theo's deep voice emerges from behind with brown paper bags brimming with groceries.

I take a grocery bag from him as he steps inside. "Wow, you mean business."

"This is the first time I'm meeting Rosie in the flesh. I need to make a good impression."

"I'm sure you have already, I've sent her a few of your notes and edits on my work."

Theo's eyes widen. "What did she say? Am I good enough for her best friend?"

"She didn't say anything. Which means she either hates or loves you, and you'll know which tonight."

Theo lets out a heavy sigh. "I better not mess up this lasagna." He produces fresh lasagna sheets, minced beef, veggies, and ricotta from a brown paper bag. From the other brown bag, he pulls out groceries that will eventually become a dessert.

"What are these for?" I ask, pointing to the shiny green apples rolling around the counter.

"A caramel apple tart," Theo says, fastening the ties of his apron.

"I thought you said you only cooked for survival," I take a seat opposite him.

"I'd like to survive on delicious food, thank you very much." He drizzles olive oil in a pot and puts the heat on.

I grin. "Fair point."

Theo begins dicing onions rapidly. Wait a minute, did he bring his own chef's knife? I know organisation when I see it. Something in my chest swirls around watching him. His knitted eyebrow, clenched jaw. My eyes slide to his bicep pushing against his skin as he minces garlic cloves. My home has never smelled of delicious food cooking on its stove tops.

"So, who taught you how to cook?"

"The culinary Gods of YouTube." His lips curve upward as he empties the tray of beef into the pot.

"Do you enjoy it?"

"Uhm, I enjoy not eating take-out or freezer meals every other day."

"I see."

"My mom had a demanding job, long hours, and that meant many lunches and dinners without her. She would leave money for us to order take out but eventually, I just wanted a home-cooked meal. And she is a great cook, but she didn't have the time to cook leave alone teach me…so I taught myself and I would experiment with everything, and my brothers were happy to be my guinea pigs."

"They're still alive, right?" I grin.

"Barely," he says, flashing a smile, keeping his gaze on the bubbling contents of the pot.

He brings a wooden spoon to his lips, tasting his sauce. Then he takes a clean spoon and scoops up some more.

He leans over. "Open up."

He places the spoon in my mouth, and a symphony of flavour engulfs my tongue. I close my eyes focusing on the earthy beef, sweet tomatoes, and fresh herbs. The YouTube Culinary Gods have taught this man well.

"Wow. And here I thought you're a one-trick wonder with the eggs." I flop the spoon into the sink, and it lands with a clink.

"As you get to know me Dawson, you'll find that I'm great at a *lot* of things." His smokey gaze pierces mine, his lip twitching slightly. Is he flirting with me?

"I'm sure," I say, my voice barely squeaking out. "I'll set the table now," I say, in an effort to change the subject.

He produces a rectangular casserole dish, from God knows where, and begins layering sauce, cheese, and pasta.

I pull open the cupboard carry out a box filled with dinnerware and place them on the chair. Finally putting my mom's housewarming gift to use. Poor woman had high hopes for her daughter. I begin laying dinner plates, wine glasses, and napkins on the table, trying to distract my mind from the 'lot' of things that Theo is supposedly 'great' at.

As I light the candles, the house fills with warmth from the scent of butter, cinnamon, and cooking apples, and the bell rings. Perfect timing.

"Rosie, James, come on in," I say after opening the door.

Theo removes his apron and comes to the door. The men introduce themselves with a handshake and I hug Rosie and then peck her on the cheek.

"Nice to finally meet you in person Theo, the pandemic has gotten me too used to meeting everyone online." She hands her bag to me, and I drop it on the couch.

Once we've all settled in, Rosie pulls me aside, whispering in my ear. "You didn't tell me he's a tall version of Matt Bomer."

"What? I don't even know who the hell that is."

"The guy from Magic Mike," Rosie says desperately as if I should have the entire cast of Magic Mike imprinted on my brain.

I glance at Theo, who is carrying the tray of lasagna to the table. "There are a million guys in Magic Mike, Rosie."

"Google it," she says firmly as if my life actually depends on what Matt Bomer looks like.

I roll my eyes.

She stays silent, her gaze fixed on Theo. "Rosie!" I urge. "Put your eyeballs back into your head."

Rosie snaps her head to face me. "Fine, fine, let's go eat," she groans.

I follow her to the table, and we shuffle around. Rosie and James sit opposite Theo and me. James begins pouring the wine.

Theo serves his lasagna, and the salad makes its way around the table along with garlic knots and roasted vegetables. The four of us eat quietly. With each bite of food, my tummy swirls in delight. "This is incredible Theo. Dibs on leftovers." I say with my mouth full.

"I have to agree Theo, I'm so happy Di won this bet," Rosie adds.

James swallows his food and turns his attention to Theo, sipping his wine. "Are you enjoying the UAE?"

"Absolutely. I mean, it was an adjustment, but I've never felt out of place. I managed to get in touch with other Americans here and we get together, watch softball and stuff. I already have a Thanksgiving invite. I miss my brothers though." Theo shrugs.

"So will they come see you or will you go back?" Rosie asks.

"We're still deciding… my brothers have school so I'm thinking of just spending the summer with them next year," Theo replies.

"I'm sure they miss you," I say, tearing a garlic knot with my teeth.

"I miss them too. And my mom. From seeing them almost every day to not at all has been the biggest adjustment."

"Yeah man, I know, my parents are back in the UK as well. Initially, I thought I'd made a mistake." James says.

"And then he met me, and realised he made a bigger mistake," Rosie says winking at him. He pulls her in by the shoulders and plants a kiss on her head.

"Nonsense, you're the best thing that's ever happened to me. No regrets."

Theo and I glance at each other and then I grin, quickly looking down at my empty plate. Something in my chest warms and twirls again. It must be the lasagna.

****

After dinner, and Theo's delicious apple tart, Rosie and James prepare to leave.

"I'm so sorry we're leaving early Di. This is the first time we left Sonia with a babysitter."

"I understand. Please smother her in kisses from me." I take Rosie by the shoulders and peck her on the cheek. "It was nice to have you over, it's been a while."

"That's because you don't cook as well as Theo," she replies.

"I'll never hear the end of it, will I?" I grin.

"Unless you can get him to cook for us all the time, probably not."

"I'll work on it." I blow a kiss to her as she turns to leave, James behind her.

I close the door and join Theo at the dinner table. He is stacking dirty dishes and gathering napkins.

"Don't worry about all this, I'll clear it up," I say, picking up the stack of plates, leaving it near the sink.

Theo raises his brow. "I'm staying." He continues clearing the table and places everything on the kitchen island.

"For what is probably the 10th time, dinner was insanely good. Thank you." The warm swirly feeling settles in my stomach as I begin packing the dishwasher.

"It was better than the pizza and Netflix I had in mind for this Friday night," Theo says handing me a plate.

"So confident that you'd win, Evans?" I pause, plate in mid-air, meeting his eyes.

"I'm still editing your book, I'm sure there'll be plenty of opportunities for me to get even."

"Hmm, just sounds like a whole lot of homemade dinners to me."

Theo grins and pulls his gaze away from me.

I close the dishwasher with my leg bumping it shut with my hip. "So, how's the job search coming along?"

Theo's eyebrows draw together as he leans against the kitchen island, folding his arms over his chest. "I guess that's one way of telling me that you don't like my work."

I laugh and prop myself up against the sink. "No, I meant that you told me you're looking for jobs in illustration."

"You remember that?"

"Of course, I take following one's dreams very seriously." Which is true. I believe that everyone should have that one thing that makes them feel alive. It doesn't have to be a full-time job. Or something that brings in loads of money. Just something you do for your soul.

"AT has a junior position that I've applied for. And I've applied for a few others."

"I hope it works out. Would you tell your mum?"

"If I'm offered the job, I will. I think she'll take it a lot easier if there's an actual contract involved."

"I hope she comes around, for your sake." I mean it. Although my parents are fully supportive of what I do for a living, I can't help but imagine how I'd feel if they weren't.

"As I've mentioned," I continue, "Rosie's parents, her mother in particular, had her whole life planned out. And Rosie just wanted out of it. First, they were unhappy that she dropped out of med school to major in creative writing and then they were upset when she married James who was 'just' an accountant. He's a Financial Advisor in a government department, mind you. And Rosie may be tough and thick-skinned, but it took years for her to stop expecting their 'eventual' approval and just do what makes her happy. I've watched her cry herself to sleep after phone calls with her parents…"

"And you were there for her…"

"I tried to be there…whenever she needed. So, when I say I hope your mum comes around, I really hope she does because I feel like she may be missing the best parts of your life or the best parts of you…and that would be a shame. For her not to see you doing something you love…"

I look down at my shoes, lacing my fingers together. Have I said too much? Is this the kind of thing that's not my business therefore I should have no say?

"You guys are a family."

"We are." I smile, my gaze staying on my feet.

Theo takes a step closer; I can feel the warmth radiating from his body. His breath grazes my forehead. He stretches his arm upward, a bit of his shirt allowing his hip to peek through. I bite my lip. Damn.

He leans forward reaching for the cupboard above my head and pulls out a glass. My throat suddenly turns dry.

I can feel his gaze on me as he brushes against me to take the bottle of water behind me. I can feel his body, barely against mine. My body, deceiving me, sends warmth up to my cheeks and neck.

He finally moves back, leaning against the counter again. "I hope I earn a spot in your family."

"You sure about that?" my lips part into a smile.

"If I can have Diana Dawson in my corner, I'm pretty sure I'll be able to accomplish anything."

The warmth in my cheeks intensifies.

"So, I have tickets to the Louvre Abu Dhabi on Monday. They're having an unveiling of their newly procured artefacts. Will you join me?"

"I'd love to," my voice croaks past the newly formed lump in my throat.

Well done Diana, you really know how to control yourself around this gorgeous man who is not your boyfriend.

Chapter 14

I clear my schedule and pencil in a lot more writing than I usually do. I have my own process. The first draft, after which I send for an edit, gives a great insight into the plot holes early on in the writing. Then I do the second draft, changing scenarios, and adding better dialogue. After a few more edits, when it is as perfect as it can be, I submit my manuscript to AT.

Theo said that he'll pick me up at five and we'll head off to the museum from here. I text him my address. After pulling up my spanks all the way above my stomach, I step into the dress I borrowed from my mum. I stand in front of the mirror, studying the floor-length emerald dress. The beaded fabric moves up to my shoulder, then falls behind in draping pleats along my lower back, leaving my back bare. My chocolate-brown hair is straightened and gathered into a sleek ponytail. A small, bejewelled dragonfly sits where my hair is tied. My make-up is minimal, with just a hint of pink on my lips.

As I place golden studs in my ears, the bell rings. I quickly open the door.

"Evans. What are you doing at my front door? This is highly unprofessional." I shake my head. Theo is clad in a navy-blue suit, the dark shade accentuating the hint of blue in his slate-grey eyes. I drink in his appearance from head to toe, trying to be subtle about checking him out.

He lets out a breath and his lips curve. "I couldn't help myself; I find myself stalking famous authors now."

"So *you're* the inspiration behind '*You*'?" I raise a brow.

Theo chuckles to himself. "I don't like to brag." One side of his lip moves up a tick displaying a half-smile. That may just be my favourite look on him.

"Are you ready?"

"One minute," I say, holding my index finger up. I hurry to the room and slip on my stilettos (no idea where mum managed to find an exact match for the dress, but it's one of her many superpowers). I grab my shimmering golden clutch purse as I leave the apartment. Theo holds out his arm dramatically, I lock my arm into him, while we walk down the passage. Just then, Lucas comes up the stairs. I pull my arm out from Theo's. The sudden movement seems to shock and offend him at the same time.

"Lucas," I croak, my mouth and throat suddenly dry. Why do I feel like I was caught sneaking a piece of milk tart before it was set?

"Diana," he says, kissing me on the cheek. "I didn't know you had plans tonight. I was thinking of coming over." He takes my hand, moving away, his gaze moving along my body. "You look incredible." I shift my gaze to my feet, feeling warmth rise to my cheeks.

"Thanks." I clear my throat and glance at Theo, struggling to find the right words. "Uhm…Lucas, this is Theo, my editor. Theo, this is Lucas, my—"

"—boyfriend," Lucas adds quickly, finishing my sentence.

Theo raises an eyebrow and says, "Interesting." A pang of annoyance nips at my stomach. Why is it interesting? Lucas could have been my boyfriend for ages.

"Theo had tickets for an event at the Louvre and asked me to join. I'm sorry." I say apologetically.

My eyes dart between Theo and Lucas. I can almost see the testosterone in the air. The men shake hands firmly, sizing each other up. Theo's face stiffens. It's the same look he'd had on his face the day we'd met in the hotel lobby. I clear my throat again, cutting into the awkward silence.

"We have to go, Lucas. I'll see you later." He leans down and kisses me on the lips for longer than is probably polite, then pulls away. Theo just averts his eyes, turning his head, completely the other way.

"See you later, babe," Lucas calls as he leaves. What the hell just happened?

We climb into the Uber. Theo finally speaks. "I didn't know you had a boyfriend."

"We just started dating," I say.

Theo studies me for a while, his gazes moving up and down. "Interesting."

I feel prickly all over, then just burst out, "Why is that interesting? Did you think that I just lived in a cold dark cave like a hermit, hunched over my laptop day in and day out, churning out books?"

He lets his gaze crawl all over me. "Maybe," he says dead pan.

I cross my arms and turn my head, looking out of the window.

He laughs. "I'm just joking. I just meant that he doesn't look like the type you would date,"

"That's quite judgmental of you."

He turns his face toward the window, and finally says, "You're right. It's not my place to say who you date."

"Exactly," I reply. What type of person does he think I should be with? If I hadn't been so mad at him, I'd be quite interested in knowing… No, I don't care what he thinks. I can date a tree and it won't be his business.

We arrive at the Louvre a short while later. The dome twinkles, giving the impression that the night sky was down here on earth to show off its stars. We get out of the car and thank the driver. As we walk toward the entrance of the museum, the water surrounding it glistens. From the entrance, the white walls reflect bright light; the cool air that sweeps our faces contrasts with the dark, sultry night outside.

People move around slowly, stopping every few moments to gaze intently at whatever catches their interest. A tour guide finds us and leads us through all the galleries, which exhibit statues and art, some of which have been loaned from renowned French museums.

After the tour, all the guests gather at the entrance where they begin the unveiling of the new items that'll be on show for the season. Once the crowd disperses, we make our way outside. We can still hear the piano being played inside. It has been an interesting evening. No matter how many times I visit the Louvre, there's always something new to see, something that has pushed the boundaries of its time, or something that is pushing the boundaries of the present.

I had forgotten all about Theo's judgmental comment until I step outside, and I decide to let it go. He is entitled to his *wrong* opinion. We listen to the music coming from the museum. The night is still, expectant. I glance at my phone; the Uber is still ten minutes away. Theo puts out his hand.

"You want to dance?" I ask him.

"Why not? There's music."

I place my hand in his, and he twirls me into his chest, his hand resting gently on my lower back, the warmth from his fingers sending a tingle throughout my body.

"I'm still upset," I say lifting my chin and putting my hand on his shoulder.

"I was wrong," he says as he twirls me again. "I'm sorry." He pulls me into his firm chest again with unexpected force.

We dance in silence. Moving side to side, him leading, me following, gracefully. It's a fun way to end the evening, even if I did step on his toes a few times. The stars glittered in the night sky. The only thing that would make this night perfect, would be if we were both single. What? Did I just think that? I look at Theo's face quickly. He didn't hear that right?

As we move around, enjoying the quiet evening, I begin to wonder what he's like around his girlfriend.

On the final twirl, I move back into his chest. He holds me there for a moment, his hand on my waist, my body pressed against his. I can smell his cologne. Sharp notes of mahogany. Subtle notes of spice. I notice the way his eye-colour changes with the moving shadows. I suddenly feel a longing for him after breathing in his scent. He studies my face and his eyes dart to my lips before gazing into my eyes again. My heart thumps in my chest. I hope he's not able to hear it, or worse, feel it. It's only thumping because dancing is a form of cardio. No other reason.

The bright lights of Uber's car shine in our faces, blinding us momentarily. making our eyes squint and we break apart. We climb into the car and remain silent for the ten-minute journey. I clamber out in front of my apartment.

"Thanks, Theo. It was a fun night. I didn't know you had moves," I wink. "And apology accepted," I smile.

Theo climbs out of the car as well. "Where are you going?" I ask.

"Please wait for me, I'll just be a few minutes." He nods to the driver.

"I'll walk you—"

"Oh, uhm, that's not necessary—"

"I want to," he says, taking my elbow gently, leading me toward the front door. I pull off my stilettos when I get in, and Theo calls an elevator. As we near the apartment, Lucas comes out of his. Perfect timing?

"Hey, Lucas."

"Hey, babe," he replies, keeping his gaze on Theo.

"Goodnight, Theo, thanks again for inviting me."

"My pleasure. I'll see you tomorrow." He waves and walks away.

Lucas turns his gaze to me. "Who did you say this guy was?"

"He's my editor," I tell Lucas, knowing well that he knows.

"I think he likes you," he says matter-of-factly.

I snort. "That's ridiculous."

"Why? You're smart," he says, kissing my cheek. "You're beautiful," he kissed my neck. "And you're incredibly sexy."

He pulls me toward him possessively, kissing me wildly. He nudges me against the wall, his arm leaning beside me, and his other hand slowly moved up my thigh, lifting up my dress. His hand passes over my knickers, which, thankfully, are lace. I imagine the mood would have been ruined if they were my 'I just want to be comfortable today' cotton ones with unicorns on them. His hand passes over and makes its way up my waist and to my back.

I heat up in all sorts of places, but Lucas's ridiculous idea is still stuck in my mind. He leans in then pulls away, scanning me, and clearly feeling hot and bothered.

"Good night." With that he leaves, entering his apartment. What the hell?

Once I settle into bed, my thoughts whirl around. Why does Lucas think that Theo likes me? If he did like me, I'd be flattered, of course. I would be lying if I said that I have absolutely no feelings for him. There is something. I felt it tonight. But I don't think I should explore further. Or is Lucas just jealous? Would that show he cares about me, even a little?

Theo had been a perfect gentleman the entire evening. Is he naturally like this? Why am I even asking this question? He's so polite and so kind every time I'm with him. Also, why would Lucas start something he didn't want to finish? Is it because he's threatened by Theo? Why did he pull away from me? Questions swirl around in my head as I doze off.

Chapter 15

I open the door and Lucas comes in with a hop in his step. He seizes me by the waist and presses his lips onto mine.

"What are you doing today?"

He marches over to my desk calendar, after grabbing a croissant from the tray on my kitchen island and tearing it with his mouth. "You should probably pencil your boyfriend in," he says, pointedly. My boyfriend runs away after he kisses me, I can't help but think while closing the door. Thankfully, I'd thrown the yellow post-it away. Otherwise, we'd be having to have a very different conversation, which would probably include me being accused of stalking.

Lucas seats himself on my work chair. I sit on his lap and put my arms around his neck. "What do you have in mind?" I ask him.

"I thought that we could join the crew for a hike." A hike? On a Monday. With his friends? I'm not sure what irks me more. The fact that he wants to do something with his friends again or that he actually suggested hiking on a Monday morning? OK, it's his friends, because I tend to be out running on most Mondays myself. I tap my finger on my chin.

"How about we do something *alone*?" I emphasise cautiously. "Let's go to Qasr Al Watan," I say quickly before he suggests anything outdoors. "I haven't been since it opened."

"OK, sure," he says shrugging his shoulder.

"And I have an idea for something we could do afterward."

He looks at me curiously. His eyebrows knit and his ocean eyes sparkle. "I'm intrigued."

I stand up and pull him up with me. "I will book tickets for later but now I have to work," I push him, with great effort, out of my apartment.

At the door, he turns around and pulls me in for a kiss that makes my mind the teeniest bit foggy. I wish he wouldn't run away every time he kissed me. My insides start to slump. When he finally pulls away, he says, "I'll see you later babe. I'm free all day."

With that he strolls away, in the opposite direction from his flat, to his Monday morning hike with his friends, I assume.

I shut the door behind me and go back to my desk, finishing the last sip of my cold coffee.

I book the tickets online and text Lucas. He'll come over at two o'clock and we'll leave together. We are going to be alone. Yes, yes, we have been alone before but the first was a fail because I ran away from him and well the second time was in my flat after a reaction, so I wouldn't call it a success either. I pace the lounge. Today is important. It may just be our first official, proper date. I don't want to put too much pressure on him, yet the pressure is most certainly weighing down on me.

I swing open my cupboard doors searching for the perfect first date ensemble. The backless black dress is not conservative enough for the presidential palace; the red dress is definitely too provocative even though my boobs look super-awesome in it. There I said it! I guess I'll save that one for an evening somewhere and he won't be able to just walk away from me after a hot kiss. I run my hand over other clothing items that Lucas had either seen or would be too formal for a first date.

I check the time. Lucas will be here soon so I have no time to Google or check on Pinterest what would make a perfect first date look. I finally settle for a cream camisole, with a champagne satin midi skirt. A cream cardigan to cover my shoulders and sneakers. I'll admit: I did a quick Google search.

When Lucas arrives, he follows me to my bedroom. He makes himself comfortable on the bed and watches me apply my makeup.

"So, what do you think?" I ask, spinning around to face him.

"You look great."

I blush, naturally looking down at my feet.

"But you should buy a better bra," he says, casually.

Had I heard him correctly? "What?" I could feel the newly-arrived colour in my face fade away.

"You know…" he continues, cupping his hands in front of his chest and jerking them upward to indicate my boobs needed a lift.

I blink and force out a laugh. I look down at my boobs. Great, he thinks my boobs are grandma boobs. Great. I'm wearing a bra. I definitely am. And a good one too. I had a La Senza sales lady tell me that my boobs would be 'perfectly perky' and 'look like I had a boob job.' I took her advice seriously but now I'm having second thoughts.

I glance at the time on my phone. "Well, I will have to do that another time. We have to go if we don't want to be late."

We got into a taxi. I couldn't help glancing at my every reflection, wondering if the sales consultant at La Senza lied to me to sell the bra, or if Lucas is a self-certified boob-ologist. I cover my chest with the sleeves of my cardigan to avoid further disapproval from any other person who sees me.

Feeling self-conscious, I'm unable to hold a proper conversation with Lucas the entire time we're in the taxi. We finally arrive at the visitors' centre. We join the queue, which is moving rather quickly, and scan our tickets.

After a security check of our bags, we're led to join a queue to get onto a bus. The bus is filled in an instant with other residents and tourists. As it starts moving, I try to let go of my worries. The bus drives around many tiered water features and vast lawns lined with trees. The majestic white palace in front of us becomes bigger and more magnificent as we inch closer. Everyone stares, wide-eyed. We park next to the wide, glistening courtyard and climb out of the bus. Lucas is quiet the entire way. He's just as fascinated as the rest of us. I knew this was a good idea.

We enter the courtyard; the marble tiles are arranged in geometric patterns. People stop to take selfies or family photos. We stare up to admire the golden calligraphy on the domes and Lucas and I snap a few selfies. As my skin starts to tingle, I hurry inside through the majestic wooden doors. I feel giddy with excitement. Like a tourist myself, the excitement and joy bubble in me, as I begin to explore an actual palace! The lobby is decorated in hues of air force blue, gold, and cream, striking a balance between traditional Arab architecture and design, and modern elegance. My jaw hangs open as my eyes widen until they can't widen any more. Then we enter the Great Hall. It literally takes my breath away. It's large enough to hold a cricket match—with spectators.

Lucas follows me everywhere we go, but smiles slightly at things I'm gaping at or mutters 'Cool' or 'Awesome' at things that leave me speechless. I feel a bit guilty for enjoying this exceptionally beautiful palace, while Lucas just hangs around. We visit the meeting rooms, luncheon rooms and a few other areas holding Emirati artefacts. Then, we make our way out quickly, clicking a few pictures of the manicured gardens quickly, before jumping on the bus again.

"So, what did you think of the palace?" I ask Lucas as he shuffles into the seat next to me.

"It was cool," he says, sounding terribly bored.

"I am sure you're going to love the next surprise!" I say holding my hands together, with a wide smile on my face, but on the inside my chest begins to tighten. Have I made this the most boring date in the history of dates? Why hadn't I googled 'great date ideas' before blurting out visiting the palace? My shoulders slump as the bus makes its way out of the palace gardens.

It's almost sunset. The sky begins to turn gold and the breeze is gentle and warm. Lucas yawns. I really hope the next place will be more to his liking. I can tell that he's thinking the exact same thing.

"On to the next surprise," he says, with little cheer in his voice.

Technically, the presidential palace was not a surprise because I'd told him about it. But perhaps his complete dislike for it was a *surprise* to him. And to me, if I'm being honest. I have little faith that he's going to enjoy what's up next, but it's too late.

I'm so out of touch with dating. I wonder if a palace tour would be on top of the 'worst places to go on your first date list.' Right now even saying palace tour out loud sounds boring.

The sun begins to set as we enter the Emirates Palace hotel which is just a five-minute drive from Qasr al Watan.

"Another palace," Lucas mumbles under his breath.

My heart sinks a little, but I pretend not to hear him.

I'm yet to find something that we both enjoy.

The taxi driver enters the gates after I inform security that we have a reservation.

Our car door is opened by the valet, and we're led to the reception lobby. The lobby and seating areas are decorated in hues of rich cream and gold, plunging us into a bubble of opulence.

We ask for directions to the restaurant. As we step outside, the sky is now cobalt blue, with just a hint of crimson on the horizon, and the lights begin to glimmer in the distance. Diners are already seated at the restaurant. The faint chatter and the scent of smoke and food fill the warm air.

After the waiter seats us, not far from the beach side, we look around us, taking in the views of Qasr Al Watan ahead of us. They'll start their evening light show very soon. And we have one of the best views.

Our menus arrive and we order drinks. To start we have a plate of beef empanadas with a spicy salsa. For mains, we both order steak and a variety of sides (truffle mashed potatoes, grilled vegetables, and a salad of grilled peach with halloumi, red onion, and walnuts, YUM!). Once our food arrives, we start eating, mentioning some of the best meals we have eaten (I had many favourites so I couldn't pin it down to just one; Lucas's best meal was a deep-fried seabass topped with sweet and spicy tamarind sauce that he had eaten in Bangkok).

As we eat, Lucas begins shifting in his seat.

After inhaling my first few morsels and feeling its warmth fill my stomach, I ask him, "Are you OK?"

"Yeah, yeah, I'm fine," Lucas says, picking up his fork, and inspecting the piece of meat on it.

"Is there something wrong with the food?" I ask him, squinting at the blob of meat, trying to figure out what's wrong with it.

"No, not really…" He trails off. He then bolts up in his seat. "Actually, this is not *Australian* beef, I mean you would think, that for the price they're charging, they'd be honest."

I eye my steak suspiciously once again. "Oh? How can you tell?

"It doesn't taste like *real* meat, you know, it's not earthy and rich."

I swallow my great-tasting meat (or so I thought).

He places the meat into his mouth and starts sucking and chewing, and then he spits it out into a serviette. Then, he slices another piece of meat and smells it, swirling the fork around his nose. Uhm. I should probably tell him that he is not sampling wine. He places another piece of meat in his mouth, and then chews noisily with his mouth open, teeth baring.

I gasp. "Lucas, what are you doing?"

Ignoring me, he continues, "See."

No, I do not want to see your chewed-up food.

"*Australian* beef does *not* have this kind of *chew*. Can't you *tell* that it's not Australian?" He leans forward, his eyes wide.

"Oh…uhm… no, mine tastes just fine," I say, shrugging my shoulders.

"Then you must be chewing it wrong," he says shaking his head, leaning back in his seat.

I roll my eyes as he looks away. Of all the things in the world that I can't do, apparently now chewing happens to be one of them.

With each morsel he swallows, he continues to lecture me. I learn how Australian beef should taste and how New Zealand beef tastes (Buttery apparently. Who knew beef could taste like butter?). I guess I now understand why some families have a 'no speaking at the dinner table' rule. Also, I am never eating steak with Lucas ever again.

****

Worst first date ever. ☹

A moment later Rosie's name blinks on my phone. I answer, immediately telling her everything, down to the boob-lifting demonstration.

"Wow," she says. "He sounds like such a snob."

"It is so strange," I say "He has never acted this way before. He was really easy going every other time we have been out together. I wonder what got into him today."

"Maybe it was just first date bad luck," Rosie suggests, in an effort to make me feel better.

I scoff. "Oh please, that's not even a thing."

We're silent for a moment.

"Or maybe," Rosie says, "he is a fisherman."

"Am I supposed to know what that means?" I ask, thoroughly confused.

"Well, yeah, you know… He used charm to hook and reel you in, but now that he's caught you, he can just pull you out of the water and chop off your head!"

"Did you need to be so visual?" I ask.

Rosie laughs, "I'm sorry, there was no other way to explain it."

"You're not gonna give Sonia dating advice are you?" I joke. Thankfully Sonia has a long time before she goes on any dates and that will give her mother enough time to come up with a better metaphor.

"Haa haa. But you get my point, yeah?"

"Yeah, yeah I get your point," I say, feeling disappointed at the thought that she is probably correct.

Picking up the sadness in my voice, Rosie chirps, "Maybe we are overreacting and maybe it was just first-date pressure and now that it's out of the way, maybe the others will be a lot better."

"That is a whole lot of maybes," I say with a sigh, feeling my shoulder hunch. I'll bet Theo and his stupid girlfriend hadn't had a bad first date.

Chapter 16

Lucas is waiting outside my door when I return from my run. Seeing the smile on his face gives me hope that the disaster date was not such a disaster after all. Not all first dates are picture-perfect, are they?

"I booked a horse-riding lesson for us this morning," he announces.

"Can we reschedule? My skin is already burning up from my run." I feel bad telling him this, but I do it anyway. Relationships are all about honesty. Even though I had started this one off with a lie, he knows the truth now so, does it count?

"You look fine," he says quickly.

"I feel horrible," I say, waiting for some understanding to come over his face but instead his gaze intensifies and his lips purse.

"We went to the castle yesterday—"

"Palace—" I interrupted.

"—palace, whatever. You owe me," he says indignantly.

"I owe you?" I ask, feeling the heat build up in my chest.

"Yes, you do. I planned this trip for us," he says, his voice getting higher.

"Lucas," I said, trying to breathe in calmly, "I. Am. Allergic. To. The. Sun." I pronounce each word carefully and slowly, practically spelling it out for him.

"Don't you think you're overreacting? Your allergy is not *so* bad."

I gasp. "I'm sorry, have you lived the better part of twenty-nine years being allergic to the sun?"

"No," he says. "But there are worse allergies out there. A *peanut* allergy could *kill* you, you know. You should be grateful."

"And you should be less of an asshole!" I said, unable to help myself. It feels good.

Suddenly my phone buzzes in my hand.

"Who is that?" Lucas asks accusingly. Not waiting for a reply, he continues, "It's Theo, isn't it?"

I glare at Lucas; I don't need to answer him. I don't want him to have another tantrum in the middle of the hallway.

"Enjoy your horse-riding," I say entering my apartment. Not waiting for a reply, I slam the door behind me.

Shit, shit, shit! I have not finished the chapters Theo asked for. Without bothering to freshen up I sit at my laptop. I type quickly, my mind fogging with thoughts of Lucas's childish behaviour, and Jamie and Isabella's issue with a murderer accomplice. I save it, not double-checking my notes. I skim over the last three paragraphs I'd just written. It's good enough for now. I hit 'send.'

I dial Rosie.

"Hey, Di. What's up?"

"I just had a fight with Lucas," I say, fighting the burn around my eyes.

"Oh no, what happened?"

"He is a child. I am practically dating a child, urrgh!" My fist tightens.

Rosie is silent, so I continue. "He wanted to take me horse-riding today. And when I said no, he basically told me that I should be grateful that I don't have a peanut allergy because those kill."

"The guy is a jerk, Diana. I don't know what else to say."

"I don't know what to do."

"You should end it. This will only end in tears."

I knew she was going to say that. I sigh. "Can't he break up with me first?" I wonder out loud.

Rosie laughs.

"Maybe I just need to give him a bit of a chance. No one is perfect," I say, not believing the words coming out of my mouth. What if my impatience and sensitivity ruin my chance at a relationship? What if it's another four years before someone asks me out again?

"Diana, he is showing you quite clearly that he doesn't respect you or your interests. James hates chess. He learned how to play just so I would have someone to play with."

"James has a brother, right?"

"Yes," Rosie answers, "he's fifteen."

"Damn!" I say, slapping my desk with pretend disappointment.

"Lucas doesn't even care enough to pretend to enjoy the things you do."

"I know, but maybe—"

"You don't have to make excuses for him, Diana."

"What if I am not giving him enough of a chance? What if I break it off prematurely?" I ask her, not expecting her to reply.

"I can introduce you to—"

"No!" I say quickly. "Please don't introduce me to any of James's 'delightful' colleagues. I love James but I don't trust his taste. Except for you, of course. That was pure luck."

We laugh as we speak about the blind date gone wrong, but we soon fall silent.

"I am just lonely," I finally admit. "I'm almost thirty. My mum's cat has a partner and I don't. I come back home to an empty home. I climb into an empty bed. I wake up and eat breakfast all alone! I just thought that by now I would at least be with someone I could have a future with."

"You can't settle for someone who only thinks about themselves Di; you definitely deserve more than that."

"I know. I've waited this long. What's a couple more years?" I say, feeling defeated. "But how am I going to avoid him? He's my neighbour."

"You're a mature adult. Things were not working out between the two of you. So, you end it." Rosie says firmly.

"What about the kayaking group?" I ask quickly, looking for another excuse not to break up with Lucas.

"You hate his friends," she says flatly.

I gasp, slightly offended that my best friend thinks so lowly of me. "I don't hate them, they're just not my crowd."

I check my phone. There's a text from Theo. That's fast.

We need to go over these chapters. Can you come by later?

No emojis. Oh no. Is he upset?

"I have to go, Rosie. Thanks for the chat."

"Any time, love. Make good choices." She blows a kiss into the phone and hangs up.

Theo texts me the address of his new apartment and I call an Uber.

Fifteen minutes later I'm surrounded by the modern high-rise buildings of Al Reem Island. It's a fairly new area, and lots more new developments are on the way, judging by the amount of red and white road barriers and half-completed buildings.

The lobby in Theo's building is bright, modern, and classy. I write down my details in the visitors' book the guard hands it to me and he checks my Emirates ID. A few moments later I'm outside Theo's apartment.

"Welcome," Theo says as he opens the door. He shows me to his dining room where I put down my laptop and bag on the dark wooden table. "Coffee?" he asks.

"Yeah, thanks."

Things feel a bit tense. He's not smiling, and thunderous clouds gather in his eyes. As he walks away, I scan the room. Minimal, in shades of stone and charcoal. Naturally Theo. Warm and inviting too, again much like Theo himself.

He finally comes from the kitchen, coffees in his hands. He takes the seat opposite me. He looks straight into my eyes, furrowing his brow. It's like being called to the principal's office. And I am in trouble.

"Are you OK?" he asks, knitting his eyebrows.

"Uh, yeah, I guess," I lie. He doesn't have to know about my fight with Lucas. I manage to smile but his expression hasn't changed so I assume he knows that I'm lying. He's the last person I want to tell that things with Lucas aren't quite going smoothly. Particularly because it'll prove the accuracy of his judgment about Lucas not being my 'type'.

"Are you sure?"

"Yeah, I am."

"OK, let's talk about this last chapter you sent me." He opens his laptop. 'Diana.' He looks at me, with concern in his eyes. "The last few chapters that you sent me were great, I enjoyed reading them, it was well written, well thought-through."

I smile.

"But." There it is. The bad news. I swallow the lump in my throat.

"The chapters you sent this morning… feel a bit rushed. The dialogue seems a bit flat, and unrealistic. And there are few plot holes that came up as well."

Heat rises to my face. I just nod. "I'll redo them," I say quietly.

"Yes, you need to," I nod again.

"By Friday, OK?"

"Yeah, sure."

As if sensing my disappointment in myself he says, "Diana, I really do enjoy reading your work. And I look forward to it as well."

He *enjoys* my writing? My chest begins to swell. No, no, no, not the point; he was just reprimanding me for my most recent flop.

"I'm sorry, I've been distracted." I know I rushed my work this morning but hearing it from someone I respect is painful.

"We can't submit that for the competition. I'm pretty sure Rosie would kill me." He says attempting to lighten the mood.

"I'll do better, no distractions." My hand slices through the air.

My eyes scan the dining room again. "So, you just bought everything again?" I ask, judging by the lack of brown cardboard boxes and mess. The flat still has a faint scent of fresh paint.

"I had some of my clothing and stuff shipped over. When Hilary and I moved in together, we got rid of some stuff."

"Hilary?" I jerk my head. There must be thousands of Hilarys in the world. It shouldn't bother me that Theo's girlfriend's name is Hilary.

"Yeah, my girlfriend."

"Is she going to move here, eventually?" I have to ask. I have to know.

"I don't know, she likes the US, we are trying to make a long-distance relationship work, but it's been hard because of the time difference."

My insides evilly gloat at the news. Hard, you say?

I stand up to take a closer look at the drawings Theo has framed above his couch. They're all signed by a Nicholas Evans, who I assume is his grandfather. "Your grandfather is really talented," I peer closer at all the fine line work on each picture. "I guess he didn't teach you much after all," I tease.

Theo chuckles to himself, "That's why none of my stuff is framed. My interior decorator didn't think the stick figures worked well," he jokes.

"That reminds me, I have something for you." He leaves the room. A few minutes later he walks out, holding a rolled-up bit of paper. "I hope you like it," he hesitates.

I unroll the paper. It's a picture, of a woman, me, in an evening gown, standing outside the Louvre Abu Dhabi. Everything around the dark-green figure was shaded a neutral grey. I inch closer to the picture. On her brown hair, balances a deep yellow dragonfly. Warmth fills my cheeks, and my stomach tightens. "Wow, Theo, this is beautiful. Thank you." I smile. Fighting the urge to hug him, and kiss him, I quickly pack up my bag and laptop.

"So, I will have the chapters to you by Friday, and thanks again for this," I say gesturing to the rolled-up paper in my hand. Just then a text from my mum buzzes on my phone.

```
We're having a braai tonight, please bring garlic
rolls.
```

My gaze meets Theo's. "How do you feel about the South African version of barbecue?"

****

Theo and I are welcomed by the faint scent of smoke that wafts through the house. "I'd apologise for my family, but I love them the way they are, so instead I'll wish you luck. And I hope you're hungry. My mum will most likely pile a lot of food onto your plate and if you don't eat every single thing, you may just as well ask her age." I tell Theo.

"Wow, OK, noted. I think can handle anything they throw at me."

"We'll see about that."

"What do you call barbecue again?"

"*Braai.*"

"*Braai.* I need to remember that."

We walk out to the backyard. The sun is turning orange and the twinkly lights draped across the garden table are switched on. Dad begins lining up *boerewors* on the *braai* stand and mom is laying out the table.

"Diana, sweetheart, you're early," Mum calls out. "Oh, and you brought a handsome young man with you." She tucks her hair behind her ears and smooths out her apron. "You must be Lucas; Diana has told us so much about you!" Theo's face slowly turns into stone.

"Mum, no," I say, between gritted teeth. "This is my *editor*, Theo Evans," I remind her. "And I don't talk about Lucas that much," I say, jutting out my chin, and folding my arms over my chest.

Theo flashes a toothy grin. "Hoo-gaan-deet, Mrs. Dawson." I stifle a giggle, but my heart lights up.

"All good, sweetheart, and don't speak Afrikaans, honey, you'll hurt yourself," she taps him on the shoulder.

I smirk at Theo whose face is drained of colour.

I lead him to my dad who's now removing the sausages from the fire and laying out the lamb chops.

"Hey, Dad," I hug him and peck him on the cheek. "I want you to meet Theo, my editor."

"*Howzit,* Theo… nice to meet you." Dad holds out a coal-stained hand to Theo. "Grab a drink and make yourself home, the food will be ready *now now.*" Theo looks at me, puzzled. "He means in about fifteen minutes," I clarify.

"Why didn't he just say that?"

"It's a South African thing."

I take him through some of the traditional sides that are laid out on the side table. *Roosterkoek* and roasted *mielies* are piled high on rectangular wooden boards. Then, in matching vibrantly painted bowls there's *chakalaka,* potato salad, and coleslaw. We fill our plates and make our way to the table. The sky turns into a pale mulberry shade of purple as we settle down on the wooden garden chairs around the matching table. Sam emerges from the house as well and joins us at the table.

"Wow, Diana you finally brought a guy home. Mum has been worried about you," he says, raising his eyebrows. I glower at Sam, kicking his leg under the table.

"Ow!" Dad groaned in pain.

I wince. "Sorry, Dad, I had a…cramp."

I turn to Theo, trying not to read anything on his face. "This is my brother, Sam."

"Nice to meet you," Sam stood up to shake Theo's hand. "I hope you enjoy the *braai.*"

Theo smiles, "I'm sure I will."

"So, what do you think of Diana's books?" Sam asks, putting a forkful of potato salad in his mouth. I can almost hug him for asking the question I didn't have the guts to ask Theo.

"I love them, I'm both fascinated and disturbed by your sister's mind." He glances at me with a half smile. Something in my chest wiggles about.

Mum carries the tray filled with meat and sets it down on the table. "OK, guys, let's tuck in." She looks at Theo warmly. "Allow me?" She gestures to the tongs and fork, to dish out for him. And he nods. He glances at me from the corner of his eye as mum places a mountain of food on his plate.

"I warned you," I giggle.

"So what are these?" he says pointing to the *roosterkoek.*

"It's bread, made on the fire."

Theo makes his way through everything on the plate, every now and then asking what things are so he'd know what he was eating. Plates and crockery clink, and we exchange stories about our lives in our home countries.

Theo leans back in his chair. "The 'brine' was really good, Mr. Dawson, very different to our American barbecue."

I shoot a glance at my Dad who catches my eye and smiles to himself.

****

"He seems like a nice guy, he's very sweet." My mum chimes into my ear as I pack the dishwasher.

"And he's taken too."

"I don't see a ring on his finger," she passes me more plates.

"Mum, no, that's like the worst advice ever; he belongs to someone else."

"I'm just saying…maybe he will be worth the fight…" She shrugs. "Did you tell him that you are allergic to the sun?"

"Yeah, I told him that time we went to the desert."

"Really? You never tell people about it…It explains why you are so calm around him."

I think about it for a moment. It was easy for me to be myself around him because he already knew what I thought was the worst part of me. "Yeah, I know, I was surprised myself… it just felt easy. I guess because there was no pressure…it wasn't a date so I wasn't scared that he may be repulsed."

"I'm supposed to feel this way around Lucas, right? He is my boyfriend. And he knows about my allergy, too."

"Darling…when it comes to love, you feel it with your heart, not your head. Love is never about what seems right or makes sense or what's logical. Remember that."

Through the kitchen window, I watch as Dad gives Theo a crash course in woodchopping.

110

My mum squeezes me tightly. "Theo or Lucas or whoever else, the right guy will find you, or him. I know you're afraid, but do not settle for someone who doesn't bring calmness, and a little bit of chaos, to your heart."

I hug my mum, grateful for her words, always. "Now let's take the dessert outside before Theo chops his hand off." She says, with slight concern in her voice.

We carry the *malva* pudding and custard and tubs of ice cream to the table.

"Diana, if that's more food, you're going to have to roll me out of here." Theo groans.

"I'll do whatever I have to, but you have got to taste my mum's *malva* pudding." I hand him a bowl with a generous helping of *malva* pudding and custard.

He spoons the warm pudding into his mouth. "You know what, walking out of someone's house is simply overrated," he says with his mouth full.

We eat the pudding and chime compliments to my mom who tucks her hair behind her ears and smooths her apron once more. Even in the dim lights outside, I can see her face turn a light shade of pink.

After we clear up, I sit outside on the garden swing, sinking my feet into the soft, cool sand and replaying the night's events. Theo and Dad are in the lounge discussing the differences between rugby and American football.

When they're done, Theo finds me outside. He sits down on the swing next to me. All the nerve endings in my body are suddenly aware of Theo's firm, lean thigh against mine, his arm against my shoulder.

"So, you didn't bring Lucas to meet your parents?" he asks. I don't think I'm imagining the slight glee in his voice.

"You caught that, huh? You seem to be enjoying that little bit of information," I scoff.

He laughs. "Not at all, it was…interesting though."

I nudge him gently. "It's complicated."

"I have the whole night."

I sigh. "I never brought guys home because my relationships usually didn't last longer than the second or third date…and then after a while, I just stopped dating all together…or if I did date once in a while, I just kept that part of my life separate…I know it sounds weird…I mean, I've told them I'm dating, but they don't force me to bring him home or anything of the sort."

"You've dated complete assholes, Diana. If they can't see that you're so much more than just your sun allergy, they don't deserve a chance."

"Sometimes I wonder if I use my allergy as an excuse. To not be out there. To not have to deal with the inevitable end. I just…I'm scared. It's like I can predict the end of each relationship…"

I push the sand forward underneath the swing with my feet.

"What about you and Lucas?"

"I don't know…he's really not my type. And I've tried to keep an open mind."

"I was wrong about what I said that night we went to the Louvre, Diana. You know, opposites famously attract."

"Sometimes they do… But I don't think this is one of those times, but I feel like I'm the one making all the sacrifices." I turn my gaze toward Theo, surprised to meet his ashy gaze. He tucks stands of hair behind my ears and a mild shiver runs down my spine.

"I hope you don't mind that I brought you along," I say cautiously. Have I shared too much with a co-worker?

"It was nice to see another side of Diana Dawson."

"Thanks for trying to learn a tiny bit of Afrikaans."

"Ah, it was nothing, a little Google went a long way. But, your mom doesn't approve of my Afrikaans. I feel hurt."

I study his face. The stubble along his strong jaw, his ashy eyes changing to the colour of smoke in the shadows. His lips, full and probably soft, break into a half smile. With great difficulty I pull my gaze away, clearing my throat, hoping the swelling in my chest would go away.

"We should have a 'brine' again. Maybe invite your parents over," he wonders out loud.

"Theo, they're not going to come over if you keep calling it 'brine'."

"You said—"

"I said *braai*!" I tilt my head back in laughter.

Chapter 17

I ring the bell of Theo's apartment. My palms are sweaty, and I've resorted to pocket tissues to keep my armpits dry. I just hope they don't fall out through my dress.

My final draft is ready. It just needs one last proofread by him. I should not be trying to impress him, but some of the last few chapters I sent him were basically shitty. I rewrote them and he was happy with it, but it doesn't feel like enough. OK, maybe I'm trying to redeem myself a little bit. I mean, writing is my only actual talent unless you could call planning and organising and stressing about not being organised enough or having enough back-up plans to your plan, a talent. I'm aware that he's looking out for me and being honest like any good editor should. I need to put out my best work for this competition.

My only excuse is that I've been thoroughly distracted. I can't stop thinking about Theo after the *braai*. There. I admit it. Although Theo and I have a professional relationship, I feel like we are growing into friends, too. I hope it's not one-sided.

Then there's Lucas. I'm not entirely sure what I am doing with him. But over the last few days, I've been in full work mode, except for the times I checked my phone to see if Lucas had called or texted. Which he hadn't. I expect an apology from him and I'm still waiting for it. But most of the time I manage to block him out of my mind.

I'm really beginning to question my judgement when it comes to men.

The door swings open, disturbing me from my ruminating. Theo stands behind it and gives me a friendly smile. My heart jumps. He's in a good mood.

"Hey, Di, come on in. There's someone I want you to meet."

I stop in my tracks, my brain trying to make sense of the sight in front of me. My eyes are wide, unable to blink, my breathing is now shallow and rapid, and my cheeks heat up.

Hilary Dupont.

Year twelve, the final year of high school. A daunting, terrorising, and stressful experience for some, while being the prime time of others' lives.

The fundraising committee usually held an auction at the end of the year to raise money for local charities. We would auction parent getaways, day trips, and concert tickets with VIP access.

The head of the committee had moved away to a school in England, hoping it would better her chances of getting into Oxford, so the spot was open. Naturally, the deputy head, me, assumed the role while searching for a new head. The deputy's head was the person who would do the admin, organising, and planning, which I loved. The head had to be a spokesperson; they had to have a way with words. They had to be able to convince people to donate, making it seem like it was their idea, to begin with. I was comfortable in the shadows, with my head down while organising the most amazing events for the students and parents.

In the middle of the year, Hilary Dupont joined our class. Her long black hair flowed like a shiny black waterfall—it wouldn't even frizz on a humid day—as she chatted with everyone, becoming instant buddies. Her energy would light up an already-lit room. She spoke convincingly; she was sharp with her words and people loved listening to her speak. In the next few months, she quickly rose from hot new girl to captain of the volleyball team, the swim team, and the debate team. She was an all-rounder in everyone's eyes but she was 'too nice' to be a threat.

We were acquainted because she was in my class.

One day, I walked up to her, as she filled her bag with books from her locker.

"Hey, Hilary."

She closed her locker, flipped her glossy hair back, and scanned me from head to toe. The first thing I did was pat down my hair. How she managed to keep her hair down and still be productive during the day was beyond me. My hair would first frizz up, then stick to my face and get into my mouth.

"Bonjour, Cherie," she said in perfect French. Her lips were full, her eyes blue, her skin pale and flawless. The black mole above her lip just enhanced all the features around it from her lip to her nose to her high cheekbones. If she was wearing any makeup, you would never be able to tell.

I took a deep breath. I'd been rehearsing the perfect way to ask her to join our committee but all that came out was: "Would you like to be head of the fundraising committee?"

She looked at me curiously. "I thought you were the head."

"I'm acting head, while I find the perfect candidate to fill the spot." I smiled, as I gestured my hand toward her.

The bell rang, signalling the end of break; she zipped up her bag and swung it over her shoulder. "I'll think about it," she said as she walked to her next class.

I would take it. It was not exactly the yes-of-course-it-sounds-like-a-perfect-opportunity-for-me-and-I-wish-you-had-asked-sooner reply I had imagined, but it wasn't a no.

The next morning, she found me in the library finishing up an article for the school paper.

"I'll do it!" she said brightly.

"Brilliant! Thank you!" I said.

"Oh no," she said, "thank *you*! I've just heard that every year the auction was held in the boring school hall—all formal and a total snooze fest."

Wait. What? Who had said that? It was a freaking black-tie event. The girls and boys loved showing off their parents' wealth that night.

I stayed silent, as she continued, "This year we can change it up a bit. When's the next meeting?"

"Tomorrow afternoon," I told her, feeling thoroughly demotivated. I'd thought the end-of-year auction was something the students looked forward to. Had that all been a lie? Were the smiles and posts and encouragement to do it again just a lie or an imagination?

"I'll have my presentation ready!" She turned around flipping her perfect hair and walked off.

I shook off the feeling of failure and finished up my article.

The next afternoon, when I entered the boardroom, Hilary was already there, connecting her laptop to the projector. She was testing it and made amendments to her PowerPoint presentation. She quickly moved through a couple of slides, scanning them for anything else she would like to adjust. There were graphs and pictures and bold red lettering saying 'NO' across certain parts. She'd really gone all out. Someone really hated the 'snooze fest.' I was also quite impressed that she managed to prepare so much in the little time I gave her. I had made a good choice to ask her to head our committee.

"Bonjour, cherie," she said, without lifting her head.

Before I could reply, the rest of the committee joined us, filling the seats around the table. Hyun-Joo took out her laptop, ready to take down the minutes of the meeting.

Hilary pushed her chair back and stood up.

"Hello, everyone. In case Diana hasn't already mentioned this to you, I am the new head of the fundraising committee. Thank you for trusting me"—she put her hand on her chest— "With this role. I will make you proud."

She commanded the attention of the room, but come on, she was not the bloody president of the country. I glanced around the room. They all seemed in awe of the person in front of them, lapping up her words. I rolled my eyes.

Then she continued. "So, word has been that the black-tie idea is beginning to bore some of our students." She pressed the button on the small remote in her hand, and a screen with the black bowtie on a white background appeared. Then at the next push of the button, big red letters 'no' splashed across the bowtie. Dramatic much? I rolled my eyes again.

Everyone in the room looked at each other, seeming a bit confused. Like me, it was the first time that they had heard that the black-tie event was not what everyone wanted.

"So, this year we are going to do something completely different. Something fun and casual."

She put up a picture of Wathba Lake.

Addy, the treasurer, lifted her hand.

"I'll take questions after my presentation," Hilary said, speaking as if Addy was a six-year-old child. "We will make it a family affair. Get everyone involved."

She clicked through each slide, showing off each of her ideas—catered picnics and BBQ, ticket prices varying on which one the family chose. Jumping castles, balloons, popcorn stands, rides. She showed us statistics of schools raising more money when the entire family was involved versus exclusive events.

There was only one problem. It was in the bloody sun.

No one in the school knew that I was allergic to the sun. I had taken part in enough extra-curricular activities that warranted being indoors that no one questioned my absence from most outdoor activities.

A medical certificate for my allergy was in my school file. It was confidential. High school is unforgiving. When people find out the tiniest imperfection about you, they use it against you, for the rest of your life. They forget everything you were or still are, and focus on your flaws.

I'd played in the shadows my entire life. I could not let Hilary ruin my last year of high school even if it was unintentional. I had to challenge her on every point. She had ideas for getting sponsors as it would be great exposure. She would be able to rope in the national newspaper. Her family knew people there. She had answers to all my questions. She began to get a bit agitated, at, perhaps, the thought that I did not swallow her idea completely. I couldn't, I was desperate not to be exposed.

I had exhausted my questions. I needed to think of something quickly. Then I blurted out. "The Emirates Palace has agreed to host us for an evening."

Hilary's face stiffened. I continued the words spewing out of my mouth like a well-thought-out, well-prepared presentation. "The idea of a family day at the lake is brilliant," I said looking at Hilary, making sure to acknowledge her effort. "But our families do these things on their own. An evening under the stars at Emirates Palace, by invitation, will make the evening special, one of a kind, a moment not to be missed. Not all our families readily turn up to the palace." Heads nodded around the room. I was making a good case, too. Without the PowerPoint. Amazing, the power of your mind, when you need to survive.

Hilary looked around the room, as worry flickered on her face for a moment.

I cleared my throat. "We have to take a vote. Majority wins."

Hilary smiled, gaining back her confidence. I'd got to hand it to her; she really believed in herself.

"All in favour of the auction being held at Wathba Lake, raise your hands."

Hilary and three others raised their hands.

I had really been expecting more hands, in all honesty. I'd loved the Wathba idea, don't get me wrong, but as co-chair of the committee, you need to be seen bringing it all together. But. You know. The sun.

"All in favour of the black tie at Emirates Palace."

Four others raised their hands, and slowly so did I.

Hilary scowled at me for a split second and then forced a smile. She was breathing deeply but trying to hide it. A vein in her forehead popped out and pulsed steadily. She was seething. She just needed some horns and a matador to wave a red flag and she would be ready to charge. But after a moment, she seemed to shake it off and resume her bubbly infectious personality.

"Well then, we have a decision," Hilary said, trying to keep her voice neutral. Her smile was plastered to her face. She shut her laptop closed and put away the projector as everyone packed up and left.

I gathered my things and turned to leave, but Hilary blocked my way. She came close to me and spoke in a tone so low, it might as well have been a whisper. "You asked me to be head of this committee. Then you shot down my ideas in front of all your nerdy friends. I'll head your boring quest for philanthropy, but you should watch your back."

She lifted her head back up and quickly composed herself. She turned to leave and then turned back to me with a smile. "Add me to the WhatsApp group, OK? *Au revoir*."

Then she left. I knew it was a shitty thing to do. To be fair, when I'd asked her, I had not expected her to make changes that were detrimental to my health. And I'm pretty sure I just wrote my name down in Hilary's bad books.

By the next day, she had managed to rope the principal into her lake idea. She was as happy as a toddler with a new toy.

Later that day I asked the principal why he had changed his mind, given the fact that he'd thoroughly enjoyed last year's event. An image of him doing a jig on the dance floor unashamed, enjoying himself a bit too much, came to mind. He murmured something about it being a great idea then quickly ushered me out of his office. Later that day I found out that Hilary's father had made a large donation to the school.

She would stop at nothing. Thankfully the Emirates Palace hadn't actually promised anything. I should be relieved that I didn't have to beg at the door of the Emirates Palace for a place to hold a fundraiser. An image of being carried out, kicking and crying by security guards while I begged for a banquet hall popped into my mind. But now I had to be part of setting up this lake picnic thing and it was not going to be a 'picnic' for me.

Hilary took charge of the rosters. I did all the admin, organising food and entertainment. Tickets, and sponsors, all fell on my shoulders. Other people would have tried to explain their circumstances, expecting empathy. I was not about to tell Hilary Dupont, who probably hates me now, that I was basically a vampire. If only the super-strength and super-speed came with it. Never let your enemies know your greatest weakness.

The day of the family picnic fundraiser at Wathba Lake was a Saturday. Rosie and I arrived early at the lake to receive food trucks and all the entertainment that needed to be set up.

At seven a.m. we went straight to the changing rooms to pack away our things in lockers.

"Did you bring your antihistamines?" Rosie asked as if checking off a mental checklist.

"Yes," I replied monotonously.

"And your sunscreen?"

"Yes, and I applied an extra layer, Mum," I said in a bored voice.

Rosie chuckled. "That's a good girl," she said patting me on the head.

I rolled my eyes. "Do you have my extra stuff with you?"

"Yes, but Di, are you really going to need an extra bottle of SPF and antihistamines?"

"I don't know, I haven't been out in the sun for a whole day in years. We are in unknown territory; I'm just preparing for the worst."

Rosie stuffed our bags into the lockers, and I gulped down an antihistamine. We walked out. "The last time I was out in the sun for a whole day was for Amelia's birthday." I shuddered at the memory.

"Oh yeah, I remember that. Poor girl was happy that her cake finally arrived only to have you faint and take all her attention away."

"I feel bad enough already, Rosie," I said, dead-pan.

We made our way down to the lake to set up the tents.

"You didn't even know you were allergic to the sun at that time."

"Try telling her that the next time you see her, I still don't get an invite for her birthdays."

"I don't think we're missing anything." Rosie winked.

"Why don't you go?"

"Solidarity, sister!" she said and pumped a fist in the air.

About an hour later, Hilary and a few of her minions arrived as well. She was in a good mood, delegating wherever she could but also trying to be involved in setting up, more so in front of the photographer for the school newspaper.

Too preoccupied to be irritated by her presence, I carried out my tasks one by one, scratching them off the 'to-do' list. I checked the time. Two hours had gone already.

"I'm going to take another tablet. I can feel my neck and arms beginning to itch a little, I'll be back." I told Rosie. She nodded and I jogged all the way to the changing-rooms.

I was about to unlock my locker door when I realised that they were already open. Funny, I thought Rosie had locked them. I rummaged through my bag for my medication. Nothing. I could feel my chest beginning to feel heavy. I went through Rosie's bag. No tubes of cream, no bottles of pills. This was bad. Even my back-up plan had failed. Things didn't just disappear into thin air.

I ran out of the changing-rooms to find Rosie. "Rosie, I can't find any of my meds or the creams," I told her, trying to hide the panic in my voice.

"What?"

She turned around, panic in her eyes. It did not make me feel better. I had hoped she actually knew where they were.

"Someone took them," I said, with urgency in my voice.

"Are you sure?"

"Of course I'm sure! They've disappeared! The lockers were unlocked."

My eyes darted around in desperation. My skin began to tingle slightly. Who would take my things and why? My wallet and things of actual value were still in my bag. Then I caught Hilary's gaze; she was watching the commotion from a few metres away. She winked and then pouted her full pink lips.

"Hilary took it," I told Rosie.

"What? How do you know?" she turned around to look at Hilary, who gave us a little wave, a big pink smile still stuck to her face. "What are we going to do?"

"Nothing," I said defeated. "I am going home; you stay and finish up and enjoy the picnic." There was a surprising calmness in my voice. Now you know what happens if you mess with Hilary Dupont. Can't say I didn't deserve it.

I'm guessing she overheard the conversation between Rosie and me in the changing rooms and used it to her advantage. I did not anticipate how low she was willing to go. There was nothing I could do now. My skin started to prickle some more. I could feel my neck heat up and parts of my body started to itch. I could not let people see me like this. I was unbearably uncomfortable.

I ran back to the changing room, grabbed my bags, and took the first taxi that arrived, back home.

Chapter 18

The week after the fundraiser, the principal kicked me off the fundraising committee because I'd 'dodged' the event, and it showed my 'disrespect' for others and their ideas. I just accepted it and moved on. No committee was worth exposing myself to everyone in the school.

On the bright side, almost every student I spoke to had asked me why we had not gone with the black-tie event. They had either been looking forward to it, or eyeing a limousine for hire, or a dress to buy. Apparently, when Hilary had come over to ask them about the past fundraising event, everyone had agreed that they had loved my idea of a black tie event and were looking forward to it this year. Talk about disrespecting others' ideas.

While it made my heart full that my idea was indeed the better one, it was too late. I was eventually thankful for being kicked off the committee. I didn't have to see Hilary's face unless it was absolutely necessary.

Until just after the winter break. I had left Math class early. The corridors were still empty, it was about ten minutes before the start of the next lesson. As I walked, I saw a folded piece of paper not far from the lockers. I unfolded it in my hands. In sloppy handwriting, there was a note. For Hilary.

My dear Hilary,

I am really sorry about the way you found out about your father and me. I wanted to tell you, I really did, but your father was not ready. He was afraid that you may not accept me. He wants to divorce your mother before making our relationship public. I am still your friend and I still care about you deeply. I understand that you no longer want me as your tutor, but my love for your father, and you, grows each day. I hope that you can find it in your beautiful heart to forgive me.

All my love, Rita

I read the letter twice more making sure my eyes were not deceiving me. My face filled up with warmth and the lump in my throat was for Hilary. I felt sorry for her.

The bell rang, and students poured out. I quickly closed the note and clutched it tightly as my eyes searched for Hilary. She walked out of the classroom, her hair flowing, her infectious smile making everyone around her happy. I walked up to her. She scanned me from head to toe. I immediately patted down my hair.

"Diana," she said with a smile plastered on her face, "What do you want?"

"I found this…" I handed the folded note to her. The smile dissolved from her face as she looked down at the familiar piece of paper.

"Did you read it?" she asked quietly.

"Yes…" I tried not to show any pity on my face.

Before she could take the note from me, Abe Langdon, the class idiot, snatched the note from her hand.

"Love letters hey Diana, I always knew," he winked as he opened the note. I rolled my eyes. His gaze moved down the page quickly and his smile grew bigger and bigger.

Suddenly he roared. "Yo! Daddy Dupont is having an affair!"

Everyone turned to look at Hilary with pity. Then he added, "With her tutor!" Everyone in the corridor burst out with laughter, pity long forgotten.

Hilary glared at me through tears that pooled around her eyes.

"I-I-I'm so sorry Hilary," I stammered.

Her face had turned beet-red. She tried to snatch the note from Abe, but he was too quick for her. She pushed passed me and went to her next class.

The next day Hilary Dupont was transferred to a new school but the news of her very famous father's affair and subsequent divorce was made public over the next few months. I had reached out to Hilary over text, email, and Facebook, apologising, but with no reply.

Chapter 19

"Diana Dawson. It's a pleasure," she says brightly, her eyes glistening. She sticks her hand out.

My mind jerks back to the present. No, it can't be. She looks the same. In fact, her beauty has matured like cheese that matures with taste over time. Or anyone who ages and looks better. Like Chris Hemsworth. I pinch myself ever so slightly just to make sure I am awake.

"Hilary," I finally manage. My voice is raspy and my mouth is dry.

Theo does a double-take. "Do you know her?" he ask, his eyes darting between me and Hilary.

"Yes. We were in a senior year together." The words struggled to leave my dry mouth.

"That's great!" he beams.

I clutch my chest, trying to soothe away the heaviness. What the hell is she doing here?

"So, how are you?" I ask.

"Well, you know, as a child of a public divorce, I am actually OK. Thanks. How are you?" Her voice is smooth and silky. Theo looks at her curiously after her public divorce comment but shrugs it off. Guilt fills my stomach and rises to my chest.

"Now that we're all here, I want to share some good news. I am going to be on the panel of judges for the Arabian Festival of Literature. Isn't that great?" she squeals and her face brightens up.

"That's brilliant, babe!"

Theo pecks her on the cheek. "Diana is entering, actually," he says, matter-of-factly.

"Yes, yes, I remember you mentioning it a few weeks ago," she nods. "It wouldn't be like a conflict of interest, would it?" She cocks her head and looks at me with a familiar glee in her eye.

"Of course not."

"Babe, did you tell Diana that I was the one who told you to apply for the job?"

I shoot a glance at Theo. She what?

"You what?" my voice strains.

"No, but—" he stammers.

Everything hits me in slow motion. The bile rises in my throat.

"I have to go," I croak, swallowing the acid burning my insides. I turn on my heel and leave the flat.

"What? Wait! Diana!" he calls after me.

I cannot believe it. Theo's girlfriend is beautiful but mean-streak Hilary from high school. It's been years since I've seen her. I've completely forgotten that she existed for a while. Is she still upset about what happened in high school? It's as ridiculous as it sounds. Theo…everything about him is just a pretence. I just don't understand why. Do they want to sabotage my career? Will it be payback?

My heart is actually sore. Or maybe it's my chest. Something in that area is hurting. Like something has been violently ripped out. I don't know what to think. It doesn't even make sense. I mean sure, unhappy coincidence that Hilary is Theo's girlfriend. And that I like him more than just friends. And that's going to add to her rage. But she doesn't know how I feel about him. But why would she tell him to apply for this job? How did she know that Theo would get the job as *my* editor?

When the Uber arrives, I jump into the car. My chest still feels heavy, the tears streaming down my face. I keep my head down as I enter my apartment building.

I dial Rosie.

"Diana, don't you think it could be a coincidence? It's a small world," she says calmly, annoying me a bit because she's supposed to be as angry and upset as I am.

"Rosie, she had literally said that she made him apply to be my editor."

"She was just pushing your buttons, Diana. Why would she make her boyfriend apply for a job a few thousand miles away from her?"

Rosie makes sense. And it explains the confused look on Theo's face.

"How do you explain Hillary sitting on the panel of judges?"

Rosie remains silent for a moment then speaks. "You should speak to Theo. Clear it up. You like him, don't you?"

"Yes," I admit grudgingly. "But, Hilary is his girlfriend. And I am pretty sure she blames me for what happened with her parents. And now I want her boyfriend too? That makes me look like *I'm* victimising *her*."

"All feelings aside, you need to speak to Theo. Get the full story before running off?"

"You're right. I've got to go; I'll chat to you later." I blow a kiss into the phone.

Why couldn't I feel this for Lucas instead of Theo? He's actually available and interested in me, I think, even if he has a funny way of showing it.

My phone rings. It's Theo. A surge of hatred, betrayal, and disappointment fills my chest. I ignore his call. I need a moment to think.

I lie down on my bed and kick my shoes off, recalling the events of the day. Perhaps the situation serves me right for wanting another woman's man. For violating Girl Code.

I breathe in deeply, attempting to calm my mind. I need to take my mind off them. I don't know what tale Hilary had spun to Theo, but it sure as hell isn't the truth. Who will he believe? No, no, no. I'm not thinking about Theo and I don't have anything to prove. I need to arrange a courier to pick up my draft. The deadline is in a few days.

My phone rings again and my eyes shoot open.

"Hello?"

"Hello, am I speaking to Diana Dawson?" A woman's voice comes through from the other end.

"Yes, this is she. May I ask who's calling?"

"I am Lizzie Anderson from the submissions department for the Arabian Festival of Literature,"

"OK,"

"I'm sorry to inform you, Miss Dawson, you no longer qualify for the competition."

"Wait… what?" My stomach knots; my eyes begin to burn.

"According to our updated rules, published authors are no longer allowed to apply," she continues solemnly.

"Oh, uhm, wow. OK, thank you for letting me know, I guess."

I call Rosie, hyperventilating, with tears burning at the corners of my eyes.

"Rosie," I pull up my knees to my chest and bury my face in them. Tears stream down my face.

I tell her about the phone call between sobs.

"OK, OK," she says, breathing deeply. "That doesn't mean we can't make this your best book yet. What if I do some extra marketing?" she continues.

As Rosie rattles off ideas in my ear, I look over my calendar and work board. It all feels completely useless now. I slump down into my chair. Everything I've been working toward for the past year is up in flames.

Unable to respond to anything Rosie says, I just say goodbye and hang up.

I leave the tears to flow with my face in my palms. There is no way around this.

Chapter 20

Everything that's happened the previous day floods back into my mind the moment I open my eyes. Theo. Hilary. Festival. In no particular order. What's done is done.

I check my phone, it's already eight in the morning. A missed call from Lucas. Argh, I'm always missing his calls. I'm a bad girlfriend— though I'm unsure if I'm still a girlfriend anymore. I'm avoiding him, and any confrontation with him instead of dealing with my problems head-on. Like adults do. Aargh.

A missed call from Rosie. Bless her, checking upon her flop of a friend. And a missed call from Theo. My gaze fixates on his name, remembering his smile, the one that makes my heart skip a beat. I can't talk to him. I just can't. Especially now that his work with me is down the drain. And of course, he may be in cahoots with Hilary.

I return Lucas's call.

"Hey." I sound as dreadful as I feel. Thankfully he can't see my face. And thankfully he isn't one of those types that just suddenly FaceTime. If you do that, you're a monster.

"Hey. Are you all right? I haven't heard from you in a while."

"Well, we did fight."

"I was waiting for your call." *You were, were you?* I thought to myself. As if I was the one being a jerk.

"I figured you were busy with work," he continues.

"Yeah, I'm sorry," I say. "I had my hands full."

"Anything I can do to help?" he asks, clearly just asking out of courtesy, from the tone of his voice.

"No, Lucas, thank you. I think I'm just going to spend the rest of the day sorting stuff out."

"OK," he replies, not sounding even a bit interested.

"Lucas, what are we doing?" I have to know where our relationship stands.

"What do you mean?"

"Well, we had a fight… We have not spoken since…I don't know if we are still in a relationship."

"Of course, we are, sure we just needed some space after we fought…Which I think we got?"

"Yeah, I guess…" I'm not sure that's the answer I want. I want permanent space. But I can't bring myself to say it.

As soon as I eat breakfast, my doorbell rings. Not being able to remember which of my online orders are arriving today, I open the door. Theo stands in front of me.

"What are you doing here?" I ask him.

"I know this is extremely unprofessional," he says.

His hair's scruffy, not perfectly gelled, and he's got day-old stubble on his face. I have never wanted him more.

Shit. No. You don't want him. Focus. He belongs to someone else.

"You don't say," I snipe.

His gaze searches mine, trying to read my mind. Not wanting Lucas or anyone else to witness this, I move aside to let him in. He walks inside and I close the door.

"I had no idea Hilary was coming this weekend. And I did not know that she was on the judging panel for AFL."

"Why did you take this job, Theo?" I just want the truth. Nothing else.

"I told you. I needed a change. Hilary wasn't happy. We decided we needed some space." There's that word again. Space.

"You said you had a girlfriend when we met."

"Yeah…I did, we hadn't broken up. We just wanted a break. And then she came down and we reconciled… and she asked about how the job was going and I told her everything…about you… I realise now that she was just prying, but I really thought she was just interested. She didn't tell me that she knew you. Only yesterday she told me that you had asked her to be chairperson of some committee in high school. She said that you didn't respect her ideas and that you turned the whole school against her and made her senior year horrible."

"What?" I can't help but shout out. "And you believed her?"

After all these years, that's the story she decides to tell. Sure, half of it is true, but I most certainly didn't turn the whole school against her. And returning the note from her father's mistress was in good faith; things unintentionally got out of hand.

"Of course not," he says calmly. He holds my shoulder and gives me the mind-reading gaze again. I shrug away.

I put the kettle on. Is it worth explaining to him what had really happened? Do I really need to relive the moment? The many moments?

"Well, I've been disqualified from the AFL competition," the words tumble out of my mouth changing the subject.

His eyes widen and he clenches his jaw. "What?"

"Someone from AFL called me," And I explain everything again.

"Wow, that's really unfair. And to change the rules a few months before your submission deadline… Cruel."

"Yeah… well," I say defeated. "I've just got to move on to other things. Focus on making this my best book yet…" I pour hot water over the teabag and watch the colour seep into the cup. "Two disasters in one week." I mumble.

"What are you talking about?"

I can't hold it in anymore. Every feeling and emotion and circumstance is bubbling and heating up inside me, like a volcano, ready to erupt. This volcano is ready to spew out its burning, hot, molten lava. Am I going to burn the people in my path?

The lava flows out anyway. "I like you, OK? You have a girlfriend, and that girlfriend is Hilary. Because of me, something that she was going through privately was made public and now I want her boyfriend? Then I'm dating Lucas. I think. Who is actually a jerk? And how does one win a competition they're not even qualified for?"

All the colour drains from Theo's face. I guess I just unloaded a whole lot of information, some of which I think is unwanted, on to him in a very short amount of time. Did I break him?

He steps forward toward me, wiping a single tear away from my cheek, keeping his warm palm there for what feels like a long time, sending a jolt of electricity down my neck to my spine. He's completely silent, his brow furrowed as he holds me in his gaze. OK, any moment now, he's going to tell me he feels the same.

And the moment passes.

Oh my God, I think I actually broke him.

He picks up the jacket he had left on my chair earlier and walks out without a word. I suppose that's one way of letting me know that he doesn't feel the same way about me, even if there are no words involved.

I bury my face in my hands. There should always be a guardian angel walking with a giant red stop sign when you're just blurting out inappropriate information. My guardian angel probably quit the day I turned thirteen.

I walk over to my door to close it, but as I reach it, it opens again, and Theo storms in, his face flushed and his jaw clenched.

"From the time I saw you taking selfies in that hotel lobby—"

Shit! I knew I was being watched.

"—you have mesmerised me. The way you laugh, the way you talk about the things you enjoy, the way you look at the things you admire. You have given me the urge to find passion in life. I want to find that passion with you… There's just something about you, Diana."

He takes me by the waist and brings me closer to him. He holds me tight as if never wanting to let go. I can feel his breath as he rests his forehead on mine. He closes his eyes and I close mine, waiting for his lips to brush against mine. He caresses my face and neck and brings his thumb to my lips, brushing it gently. A familiar warmth envelops me as I inhale his spicy scent.

"I want you, Diana, but…"

Wow, that word has a way of spoiling a moment. "But…"

"It's not the right time," he finally whispers.

My insides slump with disappointment (I really want to kiss him, and more), understanding (he still hasn't broken up with Hilary and I'm sure she won't be happy to find out that I want her boyfriend. If it were someone else wanting Theo, yeah sure, but *me*, definitely not.) and annoyance (I *really* wanted him to kiss me, dammit).

Chapter 21

Had Theo really confessed that he has feelings for me last night? I have fantasised about that very thing so many times that I can readily believe it had all been a dream.

I inhale deeply, allowing the oxygen to penetrate and calm my mind.

OK, maybe things won't be so bad. I remind myself of the pertinent facts. I don't qualify for the Arabian Festival of Literature writers' competition, but I still have a new book almost ready to be published. Also, I probably wouldn't have won in any way because Hilary is on the panel of judges and I'm pretty sure she does not want to be pals. While in no way should I have allowed my editor to express his feelings for me and hold him in very close proximity to my mouth—I would have kissed him if he hadn't been so bloody moral—

My phone buzzes, interrupting my recount of the previous day's events. It's Rosie.

"Hey, Diana. How are you?" she asks cautiously.

"I am OK," I say. It's not a lie. After my little pep talk, I've made peace with the situation.

"So, what are you going to do now? You sound a bit too calm for my liking,"

"I guess I will just send my manuscript to a new editor and submit it for printing," I say as if that had been the plan all along.

"Why do you need a new editor? What did you do to Theo?"

I gasp. "*I* didn't *do* anything!" I say. Whose side is she on? Seriously. "Theo came over last night."

"And?"

"We almost kissed,"

"And it went where I hoped it wouldn't go," Rosie sighs. "Do you need Hilary to hold any more against you?"

"It wasn't like that. He came over and he tried to explain himself to me—"

"Diana, are you sure that you can trust him? Have you cleared things up with him?"

"Rosie," I say soothingly, "You told me to clear things up with him, remember? And I trust Theo, but I don't trust Hilary… and if high school has taught me anything, she's here for her pound of flesh. Also, I spend every other day with him. I'd know if he was being dishonest."

"Why didn't he tell you he warms up to Hilary Dupont every night?"

"I don't go around asking all my colleagues the names of their loved ones, now do I?"

"You probably should, the next time," Rosie says flatly.

I laugh. "I'm thinking of getting a new editor anyway. To finish up my book. I can't work with Theo anymore. It's not a good idea to grow closer under Hilary's nose…"

Rosie stays silent. She agrees and I know she understands even if she doesn't actually say so.

"So, what are you going to do about Lucas?"

"Oh shit! I forgot about him!" I facepalm myself. "I guess I have to find the politest way to break up with him, without hurting his feelings. He called me yesterday. Out of the blue. He said he was *waiting* for my call."

Rosie laughs. "He's an ass. But good luck with breaking up with him without hurting his feelings. I've gotta go. Goodbye, love," she says, hanging up.

My shoulders hunch over. I now have to break up with a guy who I'd worked really hard to get to know. There had been actual research involved. So, research I shall turn to again.

I open up my laptop and went straight to Google. "How to break up with someone without hurting them?" Now if you ask me, pain is inevitable. Nobody likes being dumped. I browse through the articles "How to break up with someone gracefully?"

'How to end a relationship the right way?' and 'Tips for a clean break.' To summarise, you probably will end up hurting the person. I would know. I've never had to break up with anyone before. They always broke up with me or ghosted me when they heard about my condition.

I fall onto my chair, letting all the air out of my lungs.

To-do list:

1. Ask for a new editor.

2. Try to explain as truthfully as possible why your current editor is not the right fit—that one should be easy. I'm in love with an editor whose girlfriend turned out to be someone I knew in high school, who will most likely want to get back at me. Then my editor came to my apartment and almost kissed me, which I'm still thinking about, but I'm still not entirely sure if I can trust him.

3. Call Theo?

4. Break up with Lucas.

I scribble points 1, 3, and 4 on a fresh Post-it and pin it up on my board. Maybe I should call Theo first.

I pick up my phone. As I'm about to hit the call button, his name appears on my screen. I answer instantly.

"Hey Theo, we need to talk."

"Diana." He sighs. "Last night… it was… how are you?"

"I'm fine," I reply. "Last night was exactly that."

"Can I come over?" he asks.

"Yeah, uh, sure."

He hangs up immediately. It's not the way I expected the call to go, but I guess it's better to have that conversation in person.

Ten seconds later my bell rings. That was quick. Is he outside? I check my hair in the mirror and touch up my lip balm. Just in case he decides that he wants to kiss me this time. I swing open the door with my best I'm-happy-you're-here-but-you-probably-shouldn't-be-here smile.

Lucas stands in front of me. My stomach sinks to my feet. "Hey, babe." He comes forward, leaning over to kiss me on the cheek. "Do you have plans?"

Feeling a thorough whiplash, I struggle to find my words. "Yeah, I do," I say, trying to sound apologetic.

Wow. I'm blown away by this guy's ability to act like our fight the other day had never happened. Why am I still hanging on to it? Maybe because he hasn't bothered to apologise, and he assumes we just needed space.

"Will you be free this evening? The guys are having brunch at St Regis. It's phenomenal."

This will be a great opportunity. I can break up with him after we'd had brunch. Maybe he won't take it so badly on a full belly. But I'm not ordering steak, and neither should he. "Yeah, it sounds great, I will be there."

He walks around. "I haven't heard from you again since our chat the other day, what have you been up to?"

I'm about to answer, then suddenly Theo dashes through, out of breath. Oh, God. He is beautiful. That sexy stubble, those piercing eyes—

"Diana—" I jump, realising I had been eating him with my eyes. With Lucas in the room! Get a grip, woman.

He stops in his tracks. His face turns to stone and his eyes turn cold as he lays them on Lucas.

Lucas' face turns solid, too, and he curls his fists. "What is *he* doing here?" he asks through gritted teeth.

Holy crap. Jacob Black and Edward Cullen moment.

"I invited him over," I say, casually. "We have some work to go over."

"I see. So *he* is keeping you busy?" he asks as if he's finally spat something bitter out of his mouth.

"I work with him, Lucas. We spend a lot of time together. I can't help it."

Lucas turns to leave, but then stops and jerks back. He squints at the note on my board. Oh shit! I'm pretty sure he zoomed in on note 4.

"Break up with Lucas," he reads, and then sniggers. "Wow, Diana, just one of the things you had to do today, and then simply scratch off."

I bite my lip. He picks up the note and squashes it in his hand.

He walks toward me and looks at me straight in the eye. "Go to hell."

At least *I* wouldn't have to break up with *him*. Rosie will have a laugh for sure.

He storms off, nudging Theo's shoulder on his way out.

"I'll be right back, OK?" I say to Theo, securing my gown around my waist.

I run after Lucas, who is moving at an incredible speed. This was not how this was supposed to go. I need to apologise.

"Lucas," I call out. "Lucas, please wait."

I finally reach the doors leading out of the building, the cool air smacking against my face. Lucas spins around, his icy gaze sending chills down my spine.

"What do you want, Diana?" he seethes.

"I-I'm sorry, please let me explain."

My skin starts to prickle. Fuck. Of course, I'm outside, with no SPF, no antihistamine. My face begins to heat up, and I can feel my neck beginning to burn. I have to see this through. A few more minutes.

"Oh, explain why you broke up with me via Post-it note, you mean?"

"Technically you weren't supposed to see—" I break off, looking at his face. I'm clearly not making anything better. "I am sorry Lucas," I say earnestly.

"I knew you had the hots for your editor," he scoffs.

"It isn't like that," I say, trying to convince Lucas. My neck might as well be on fire now. I quickly glance at my hands. Red patches begin forming.

Lucas rolls his eyes and turns to walk away. "Wait, Lucas, I am trying to apologise." I let out a breath.

He comes close to me and peers into my eyes, his eyebrow twitching. "Apology accepted."

"OK." I half smile, "Great, can we still be friends?" I ask. I'm not sure why, but it seems like the right thing to say now. Even though I cannot imagine what that would look like.

"No," he says, flatly and storms off toward the parking lot.

That went well.

My hands and neck feel as if they're on fire, the tiny ants crawling rapidly, their minuscule feel tapping every nerve on my skin. I run back inside and shut the door behind me, catching my breath, sliding down to the floor, back against the wall.

"Are you all right? What can I get you?" Theo's deep voice pierces my thoughts.

My breath finally stabilises, and I wobble to my feet. Theo helps me up. "Thanks," I say, not quite wanting to meet his eye while resembling a ripe tomato.

I make my way to my medicine cabinet, and Theo shuffles around for a glass and fills it with water.

As soon as I gulp my antihistamine I lie down on the couch, and Theo turns the air conditioning down. The room is instantly cooler, gently blowing the soothing air all over my prickly, burning, skin.

Theo sits down next to me on the couch. As awful as I feel, his spicy masculine scent makes my heart beam and want to jump out of my chest. He takes my hand in his and studies it carefully. "You're swelling," he wonders out loud. He meets my eye. "Is it always this bad?" he asks, his eyes creasing slightly around the corners.

"Yeah…when I'm stupid enough to go out into the sun, without any form of protection."

He tucks a few strands of hair behind my ears. His gentle touch sends electricity shooting down my neck. "Lie down," he says, "I'll bring an ice pack."

I lean back on my couch. I can feel each strand of the fabric on my aching skin. Theo wraps the ice pack he found in the freezer in a clean dish towel and seats himself next to me. Carefully, he dabs the towel against my head, my skin thankful for the relief. But my body seems to be heating up against my wishes. He is so close to me. I scan his face. The fleck of blue in his grey eyes, the creases around his eyes, the frown lines crunched together on his forehead. I gaze at the shape of his lips, the edges pointing down ever so slightly. My hip is very aware of his knee nudging against it.

"You're kind of perfect." I'm surprised by my own voice as the words leave my lips. I really hope I have not just repeated a cheesy line from a chick-flick.

Theo's lips twitch, fighting to curl upward and break into a smile. "You're high on antihistamines," he says.

He dabs my forehead again, and I glance at his bicep pushing against his skin.

"It's never impaired my senses." And up until now, it's never heightened my senses either. But right now, every sense I have which I'm beginning to think is more than five, is in overdrive.

"Thank you," I smile at him.

"The swelling has gone down," Theo says, taking my hand is his again. His hand is cool, yet leaves a burning imprint on mine when he places it back down. He suddenly comes closer to my face. He tips my chin up with his thumb, and I can feel his warm breath graze against my skin. My heart is thumping against my chest, and I'm pretty sure he can feel it. He scans my neck for a moment more. His Adam's apple budges as he swallows. A second later he pulls away. "The swelling on your neck seems to be going down too."

Of course, why else would he bring his face so close to mine?

His lips curve. "You're on the road to recovery, Dawson."

"Thank you, Evans, but I'll be on the road to anger if I don't get something to eat." My stomach grumbles loudly in agreement. I begin lifting myself up from the couch.

Theo places his palms on my shoulders, pressing me down, back on to the couch. "Let me,"

I don't fight him. I lean back, allowing my head to sink back into the soft cushion. My eyes feel heavier, and I shut them, while the sound of Theo scuffling in the kitchen fades away.

****

The decadent aroma of butter wafts through my apartment.

My eyes shoot open, and I scramble off the couch. I glance at my hands and arms and touch my face and neck. The swelling is completely down, and my skin has a faint pink hue. I glance at Theo.

Theo lifts an eyebrow. "Did you just sense the food being ready? I can swear, that you were fast asleep a minute ago."

"When God was handing out superpowers, he gave a bunch of the useless ones to me." I tease.

Theo chuckles to himself and places toasted sandwiches on the table.

After I freshen up, I'm back in the dining room.

"So, what happened with Lucas?" His eyes begin to sparkle, showing off a hint of blue. Someone's enjoying this a bit too much.

"He broke up with me. Kind of. Or did I break up with him first?" I wonder out loud. He dumped me and I'm OK with that. Am I evil?

"Are you unhappy?"

I shake my head, "No, I don't think so,"

He brings me closer to him by the waist and takes my lips in his. His lips are soft and perfect on mine, I inhale his spicy scent as our lips move together, pushing and pulling on each other, wanting each other, needing each other, desperately. My body responds, like a magnet, unable to resist his body. My fingers move through his hair, his hands move along my neck and spine sending electricity through my whole body.

I pull back, but he holds on. He caresses my cheek, moving my hair out of my face. He pushes the gown off my shoulder and brushes his lips over my skin which has turned sensitive to his touch. Butterflies consume my entire body as he slowly removes my gown. I come to my senses quickly, shoo-ing all the butterflies away. With great difficulty and unwillingness, I gently push him away. "What happened to 'it's not the right time'?"

"Don't listen to me. I don't know what I'm talking about," he says, trying to rope me closer to him again.

"Theo," I say in the firmest voice, denying the fact that my legs may as well have turned into water.

"Come on," he groans.

"You are still my editor. And have you broken up with Hilary yet?"

"Yes, I have."

I move back in shock. He gestures to the food on the table. "Come on, let's discuss this over the best grilled cheese sandwich you've eaten."

Theo sits opposite me. My teeth break through the crisp, buttery bread. The butterflies that began dancing around in my stomach from Theo's words, are forced to relax after the first bite of the gooey cheesy sandwich.

"Things were rocky; we were on and off, and before I came here, I was feeling suffocated in our relationship."

I keep my gaze on him as he speaks.

"I brought it up one day that I wanted to experience living and working in another country. She supported the idea, and that's why she helped me look for jobs. I was grateful to have an understanding and open-minded partner like her. Maybe she did it because she felt the same and thought the space would suit us well. And it did."

He smiles. "Our relationship was actually a lot better when we were apart."

Hilary as a mature woman capable of loving someone other than herself. I think back to the look on her face when I handed her the note from her father's mistress. I felt sorry for her. I felt sorry that she had been betrayed, maybe, by those closest to her...I look at Theo. He remains quiet for a while, a pained expression on his face from what I assume are memories, good or bad. He hasn't touched his food.

After a while, he meets my gaze and says, "Then I flew here and met a person wearing a yellow stripy dress and I haven't stopped thinking about her since."

I knew that dress would bring me love. OK I didn't, but it would be a great story to tell the grandkids one day: When I saw this dress in the store, I *knew* it would bring me to the love of my life. Just watching Theo in his chair, enjoying his meal is enough to make my heart glow.

"When Hilary came down here, I thought things were going to be OK again, but you somehow worked your way into one of our conversations." He laces his fingers through mine. "And now I can be with the woman that makes me lose sleep at night."

My heart shines even brighter. My whole body feels as if it had lit up. But slowly my chest begins sinking, realisation setting in.

Tears burn around my eyes, fighting to flow out. "Theo," I say, slowly, hating everything I'm about to tell him. "You just broke up with Hilary, I just broke up with Lucas. Well, you know what I mean," I add quickly, looking at Theo's raised eyebrow. "We need time. OK?"

I know Theo needs time; I most certainly do not. I feel strongly for him. Do I love him? It's too soon to tell. But, my heart lights up like the sun lights up the morning sky when he's around. And it's the best feeling I've had.

I continue, "We need to take things slowly... for now, till I find a new—"

"—editor," he finishes, exasperated. "I know," he says, sounding defeated.

"Thank you for all this," I say gesturing my palm around.

He gets up, leaving his half-eaten sandwich, and leaves the apartment.

I let all the air out of my chest, bringing my knees to my face, ducking my head down, and letting the tears finally flow for as long as they need to. After a moment, I know exactly what I need to pick me up.

"Hey, Di, how are you?" Rosie's voice comes through.

"Single, once again," I sniff, then wipe my nose with a Kleenex.

"You broke up with Lucas. You actually did it!" She sounds as if she wants to give me a high five.

"Well, he told me to go to hell after he saw a Post-it note with 'break up with Lucas' written on it." I wince at the memory.

"Who would ever write that on a Post-it note-?

"I—"

"Never mind, don't answer that. I can't say he doesn't deserve it."

"Am I just never going to find love?" I ask, feeling sorry for myself.

"You found love, he's just also…someone else's love."

"He broke up with her…"

"Really? I knew I liked this guy," she says trying to lighten the mood.

I crunch my eyebrows. "No, you didn't, you were just having doubts about him a short while ago."

"Well, I like him now."

"You are mad, you know that?"

"One of my best qualities."

"Anyways, I told him we need to take things slowly."

"Oh, so what did he say?"

"I think he understands…I also feel really, really, guilty about taking Hilary's boyfriend."

"Diana, you're not taking a toy away from a child. He is falling in love with you, too."

I sigh. The guilt still is growing in me, gnawing at my insides. For ending things the way I did with Lucas, for making Theo wait, for stealing Hilary's boyfriend (despite what Rosie says).

"Di, maybe just take this as a break from everything that's distracting you, focus on your getting your book out. We can still make this a bestseller."

"You're right. No men. No feelings. Just making my next book the best I've written." I sit up in my seat and straighten my shoulders.

Fully focused work mode Diana is back.

****

I climb into bed that night, replaying all the different ways today's events could have gone. It all happened for the best, I conclude. My phone beeps and a text from Theo comes in:

```
Diana, I do have feelings for you, but, I want to
give my relationship with Hilary another shot.
    I do love her, and I owe us a second chance.
    I know you understand.
```

A weak smile forms on my face. Diana Dawson always understands. My glowing heart flickered and detached, sinking into a growing hole in my chest, deep and dark.

I curl up on my bed, tears streaming into my pillow, unable to stop my body from shaking, and somehow, I fall asleep.

Chapter 22

Alia Al Hosny's raven black abaya flows down to her ankles as her feet gently clink toward me.

"Marhaba Diana." She holds out her arm. I stand up and lean toward her in an embrace, inhaling the intoxicating scent of oud.

"Marhaba Alia, it's nice to see you again."

"You too. You hardly come into the office anymore." She says as we sit down.

"I concentrate better without Kate yelling at Anirudh for finishing her oat milk."

"She yelled at me for pointing out that her plant-based diet is making her cranky." Alia raises her perfectly shaped eyebrows.

I snort out laughter. "I should probably work from home till Kate adjusts."

The waitress jots down our coffee orders and leaves.

"I must say, I was really excited when they asked me to be your editor." Her caramel eyes twinkle in her heart-shaped face.

"Really? I didn't know you were into horror."

"I'm not. At all. Trust me. I lost some sleep after I read your first book." She bares her teeth and I immediately think of the WhatsApp emoji with the same expression.

"Oh. I'd apologise, but that's exactly the kind of thing I like to hear from my readers." I grin. "If you can sleep at night after reading my book, I haven't understood the assignment of horror novelist now, have I?"

Alia drags her chair forward. "Fair point."

"So, why are you doing this?"

She shrugs her shoulders. "I thought it might be a great challenge. Something to get me out of my comfort zone."

We hunch over the coffee placed in front of us and sip in silence.

"How is Rosie?" Alia asks, tucking stray stands of golden-brown hair back into her hijab.

"She's adjusting to motherhood. Not seeing her every day has been an adjustment for me too. I'm so used to her being around for everything. Now I just feel like a news anchor updating her on Diana Dawson's world."

"Ah it will get better; the first three months are the hardest." She pauses. "And the second. And the third, actually. It's pretty much full hands for many, many years."

"Thanks, Alia, that makes me feel loads better."

"Your success is not dependent on whether Rosie is around or not. *You* are the heart and soul of your stories. Our editors are just there to bring out more of what's already there. Remember that." A kind smile spreads over her face and her words somehow wrap me up in a warm hug.

"Thank you for saying that. That actually does make me feel a lot better."

I tell Alia about Rosie, and our unique work dynamic because we have been friends for so long. She is quite intrigued about how that worked out.

Alia tells me about her love for the English language which has always been a passion of hers, even though her mother tongue is Arabic.

When she speaks about work, her warm personality melts away, and an editor, who's driven, motivated, and serious about making you look good, shines through. Her attitude and attention to detail, not to mention her impressive organisational skills, make me bubble up with excitement.

For a short moment, I forget that I don't have a chance at achieving my dream. In fact, Alia makes me feel like it can still be possible.

Chapter 23

My phone rings as I pull the brush through my hair. I glance at the unknown number on my screen and pick up. "Hello," I say, using my most professional voice.

On the other end, a woman's voice comes through. "Hello. Is this Diana Dawson?"

"Yes, it is."

"It's Lizzie Anderson, we spoke the other day?"

"Yes, I remember." I smile, not that she can see it. I'm not sure why I'm smiling either. She ruined my life with one phone call. Scenes from *The Ring* flash into my mind. *"Seven days."* The voice whispered from the other end of the phone. I shudder at the thought.

"I've called to tell you that due to the overwhelming complaints on the updated rules for the competition, we have decided to allow published authors to apply."

"I'm sorry?" I ask, not following what she just said.

"You are still allowed to submit your manuscript for the competition."

"So, the rules have changed again?" I need to make sure I have my facts straight before allowing any emotion to flood in.

"Yes, please have your hard copy submission in by the end of the month."

This is… I was not expecting this. These guys change their minds like they change their underwear. I certainly hope they aren't changing their underwear only once in two weeks. This is a bad comparison. Stop thinking of underwear. Focus.

Lizzie's voice breaks through. "Miss Dawson? Are you there?"

"Yes, I'm sorry, this is just really surprising. In fact, I tried my best to forget about it for a while, given that I thought I had lost my best shot. Wow."

Realising that I'm rambling and hyperventilating, I stop speaking and take a deep breath." That is amazing," I continue, searching for a better word. Unable to come up with any, I am shame of all writers out there, I just finish with, "Thank you so much."

"It's our pleasure. We will see you on the 20th. Good luck," she squeaks, before cutting the call.

My chest heaves up and down, trying to contain my disbelief, shock, nerves, and excitement. I have to tell Rosie, and Theo, wait, should I tell Theo? He was my editor, too. But I don't know if I have it in me to even text him… I have to tell Mum and Dad and everyone on social media. Hell, I might even run over to Lucas's place and let him know, but something tells me that that would probably be a bad idea.

I grab my printed manuscript and shove it into an envelope. I arrange for the courier to pick it up then I text Rosie to let her know that I'll be coming over.

****

The Uber crunches up the gravel driveway and the driver barely stops when I hop out of the car. My whole body is jumpy with nerves and my face hurts from holding the constant smile on it.

Rosie opens the door. My voice comes out much louder than I had planned. "They've changed the rules again! I'm back in the competition!" I stick my arms up in the air.

Rosie's eyes light up. "What?"

She grabs me for a hug. I hold her and we both jump up and down squealing for what seems like a good few minutes. James scrambles down the stairs, hair dishevelled, in his pyjamas and flip flops, clearly surprised at the jumping women in front of him.

Rosie lets go of me. Her smile is wide as mine as she looks at James.

"She's back in the competition, babe," she says to him.

His eyes widen too and he comes over to grip us both in a bear hug. Tears of joy pool around the corners of my eyes. We finally pull apart.

"This is great news, Di." Rosie smiles warmly and rubs my shoulder.

"Well, since you're here," James interrupts, "I might as well make breakfast."

"I could eat." I grin.

Rosie and I follow James into the kitchen. "Where's Sonia?"

"She's asleep '—Rosie yawned—' thankfully. She was awake all night. James and I took turns to try to rock her to sleep, but she had plans of her own." Rosie brings the baby monitor closer to her and turns up the volume.

We seat ourselves around the breakfast table. James gets busy in the kitchen. Pancakes sizzle in the pan, the aroma of coffee wafting in the kitchen. My tummy grumbles.

"So, have you spoken to Theo?" Rosie asks in a hushed tone.

"No… I haven't…"

I haven't spoken to him since I requested a new editor. And I didn't even tell Rosie about his text. I have tried to block it out of my mind.

"I think I hurt him. And now he's patching things up with Hilary." I say quietly, looking at my palms, and swallowing the lump in my throat.

"What?" Rosie's voice booms. She pushes the chair back noisily.

James gestures "What are you doing?" with his hands. Rosie winces. "Sorry," she whispers, grimacing.

"He broke up with Hilary, for me, and then I told him that we should take it slow, and I thought he was OK with that. "

Rosie puts her hands over mine. My chest feels heavy, and the lump in my throat returns, larger this time.

"I don't understand," I sniff, "I don't understand why he would go back to her…he said he still loves her…I thought he was OK with my sun allergy." I trail off, tears rolling down my cheeks.

"What do you mean?"

"He sort of took care of me after I had a bit of reaction the other day…and it was that same evening that he told me he's getting back with Hilary…the only reason I can think of is that he saw me all red and puffed up." I bury my face in my hands.

"Diana, I really don't think Theo would do something like that. He's known you have an allergy from the time you met him. Why would it appal him now?"

Rosie takes me into her arms, and I sob, softly, happy to get it out, grateful for her support once again. I love that Rosie knows when to just listen. She doesn't always offer her advice; she doesn't feel the need to say the right thing.

"I don't know Rosie," I sniff, "it just doesn't make any sense. I don't know what else to think. And I hate that I'm thinking the worst about him."

James puts down coffee and pancakes in front of us. He carries his breakfast out of the kitchen, mumbling something about football being on. I've always liked James. I lift my head up and clean my face with a Kleenex.

"Let's eat," I say, feigning a smile. We help ourselves to the warm, fresh pancakes, taking turns to drown them in maple syrup.

We sip our coffee and eat in silence, letting the food and drink comfort our souls.

Rosie sits back and watches me carefully. Then she shrugs. "I am surprised about Theo, though, I thought he was into you, I thought he would be more understanding about wanting to take things slow. I think that may be it."

"It's just an excuse, Rose. Others have broken up with me because of my allergy. I don't think this time is any different."

I thought that we just needed some time to figure things out a bit more, how to tame Hilary in the process. I thought we both wanted the same thing, each other. But his seeing me with an allergic reaction may have been a deal-breaker for him. Will it be stupid of me to hang on to the tiniest flicker of hope?

I say none of this to Rosie. She'll try to convince me that I'm wasting my time, and she'll be right.

I change the subject before Rosie could read any of my thoughts. She has a freaky way of doing that sometimes.

"We need to get ready for the reading at AFL. Will you be able to come to Dubai that weekend?"

"Of course. I'm not gonna sit here and wonder whether you're screwing up or not. We can make it a girls' weekend." She runs her fingers through her hair and yawns again. "And, I need to get out of this house."

"Great! That will be fun. My family will most probably join us, though."

"Yeah, that's alright. As long as I'm away from mine for an evening."

I grin, draining the last of my coffee before getting up to clear the table.

Rosie puts her head down on her folded arms and closes her eyes. After I wash my hands, I bend over Rosie and kiss her forehead.

"Thank you, Rosie. I love you," I say in a small voice.

"I love you too, Diana. You've got this."

She lifts her head and smiles sleepily. I grab my bag and make my way out.

Chapter 24

The weather is much cooler so I can be outside for a full five minutes without my face melting off. I decide to walk out to the main road and hail a taxi from there. The sky is blue again (during summer the sky turns a sad shade of something trying to be blue, but not quite getting it right—thank you humidity) and the air feels lighter. Cars zoom by, as well as a few occupied taxis. A taxi finally pulls up in front of me and I get in.

"Al Raha Beach, please."

I scan the QR code to pay and wait for a second for it to go through when we arrive outside my parents' home. I'll always be grateful for being alive in the era of technology. I thank the driver and he leaves.

The aroma of cinnamon and butter wafts through the house as I enter. I arrived in time for my second breakfast.

"Hey, Mum," I chime as I enter the kitchen.

My mother is bending to take a pie dish out of the oven. A milk tart is in the making. The custard is in a pot on the kitchen table and the crust is in her hand. She lays it on the table carefully and only then does she look up at me. Mum is one of the 'overcautious in the kitchen' types. She won't look at you or speak to you if she's dealing with anything remotely dangerous. She maintains that hot pans and sharp knives need one's full focus.

After what felt like moons, she finally replies. "Hi, darling."

She comes over and pecks me on the cheek, knowing well that the stain from her lipstick will be imprinted there.

Before she can run off and start doing something else, I take her soft hands in mine. "Mum, I'm back in the competition!" A wide smile spreads across my face. I can't help it.

"That's amazing, honey! You've worked so hard. You deserve a shot."

"I thought I smelled cinnamon." Dad's voice booms behind me. Sam follows.

They're both slightly sweaty and flushed. They've been outside, in the garden, one of their ways to bond.

Mum gets up from the table and pushes them both out again. "Go wash up, please." And they obey.

"And hurry up, Diana has exciting news for us," she calls after them, with a smile that lit up her face.

When they return, fresh and clean, they gather around the table. Mum pours out coffee and brings a box of Ouma's rusks to the table. So much for a second breakfast of milk tart.

I start the story again, answering all their questions and accepting their praise. When my dad finishes his coffee, he comes over to me and pats me on the shoulder. "Turns out they take the complaints seriously, I sent them a few myself, pretending to be your attorney." His face beams with pride.

"Thank you, Dad. You're the best." I stand up and wrap my arms around him.

"So, what's next?" Mum asks, pouring the custard into the tart shell and then sprinkling powdered cinnamon generously over the top.

"I need to prepare for the public reading. I need to text Alia." I pull out my phone.

```
Hey, how are you?
```

Her reply comes in immediately.

```
Hey, Diana. I'm alright, how are you? What's up?
```

```
How would you feel about coming over to my mum's for
a slice of milk tart this afternoon? ☺
```

She arrives a few hours later, bearing a bouquet of flowers. My mum comes to the door as well as I welcome her in.

I spill the beans to Alia as we spoon milk tart into our mouths. She squeezes my arm. "Thankfully they have made their decision quickly, else we wouldn't have had any time to prepare! Let's get down to it?"

I lead her to our lounge where she makes herself comfortable across from me, pulling out her laptop, and straightening her shoulders. I seat myself opposite her.

"Rule number one of any public reading is to be prepared. I don't think you will have any problem there," she says approvingly.

"So, since this is your first public reading, there are a few things we need to do to make sure your reading is fab, not drab. You should take notes," she says pointedly.

I tap away furiously as she speaks. "Your reading should be entertaining for your listeners; you want to engage them and make them feel something all at the same time. Lengthy descriptions, set up, or back story are a big no." She crosses her hands in front of her face.

She lists a few more suggestions for making my public reading a success and then we're on to aligning our schedules to fit in reading practices as well.

I'm charged up, ready to take this competition head-on.

Chapter 25

My eyes scan my packing list, then I scribble down 'antihistamines' in capital letters. I circle the word and underline it twice. Yes, it's four weeks away, but it can't hurt to have your thoughts on paper, all organised along with your hotel booking confirmation and festival passes, and an extra copy of your application.

You never know, the guard at the entrance could be having a bad day, he could check his list, insist you're not on it, and then you'd have to show him your application form stamped 'author' in big red bold letters.

OK, my application form does not actually have such a stamp, but it gives me peace to slip it in with my other documents.

I stack everything neatly and put them into my file, which I then leave on my table. Satisfied that I've ticked off yet another thing on my to-do list—make a list of things I need to take to Dubai—I grab my bag and leave the apartment.

The elevator dings on the tenth floor and the metallic doors open. I hardly ever come into the head offices of AT but today I'm meeting Kate, my line manager, to discuss my leave for the festival and the future of my job if I win the competition. Sure, it's presumptuous of me, but it's always good to know.

The ceiling lights shine brighter than ever, something I've never grown used to in all my years visiting the building. I wave to the receptionist, who's touching up her lipstick. She waves back.

I bump into a firm chest and drop my bag, causing its contents to spill all over the floor. Great start to the day.

Cursing, I bend down to pick everything up and then I hear a familiar deep voice.

"Diana," he says, his eyes crinkling. My stomach tightens and the hole in my chest feels deeper than ever before.

I stand up and meet his gaze. He's still as handsome as the day we met at the hotel. The memory of our first meeting suddenly causes a slow burn around my eyes. I haven't spoken to him since the day I asked him to take things slowly. And his text.

He breaks the silence. "I heard that you're back in the competition. Congratulations." He smiles.

"Thank you," I say, trying not to meet his eyes.

There's silence again.

"I have a meeting with Kate —"

"Why didn't you tell me?" he says at the same time, his brows furrowed.

Unable to resist, I gaze into his eyes, which have turned to steel. I suddenly feel a pang of guilt. I should have told him. Why hadn't I? It would have been the polite thing to do, after all, he had helped me.

My chest feels heavy again. I look away. "I don't know," I admit softly. "I should have."

"Why are you doing this? Whose feelings are you playing with now? First, it was Lucas and now, me?"

I glare at him, tears filling my eyes. "Playing with your feelings? You told me that you wanted to make your relationship work with Hilary after we decided to just take things slow!" My voice comes out much louder than I expect. I glance around, at people poking their heads out, even the receptionist holding her lipstick, frozen in mid-air, watching the commotion.

Theo clenches his jaw. "What are you talking about?" His voice is quiet now, his eyes darting about the onlookers.

I yank my phone out of my bag and search for the text. Reading those words again darkens the hole in my chest even more.

He takes the phone from my hand. His steel eyes ran over the screen repeatedly. Finally, he hands it back to me. His stony expression returns.

"Ring a bell?" I ask him, offering a tight-lipped smile. I begin to move away.

He grabs me by the arm and pulls me back to him. I can feel his breath on my cheek, I inhale his familiar scent, and the familiarity, and peace I feel when I'm close to him is replaced by ache and longing. "Do you think I enjoy feeling this way?" His eyes grow stormy, and his jaw tightens.

"You've made your choice," I say still holding his steel gaze. I shrug my arm away and leave, my face hot, tears rolling down my cheeks.

I'm not interested in any excuses. Hilary and Theo deserve each other. How dare he accuse me of playing with his feelings, how dare he demand anything from me? He made his choice. He chose *her* over me. And that was it. I don't need to know why. I have nothing more to say to Theo Evans. I bury the hole in my chest and dry my tears. I'm here to become a New York Times bestseller. And I'm not letting a guy who can't make up his mind get in my way.

I walk straight to Kate's office, drying my tears with my sleeve. I have no idea what got into him. He is acting like I broke up with him. How could he turn this on me and play the victim?

"What was all the fuss about out there?" Kate's voice pipes, disturbing my inner ranting. She's typing away on her laptop, muttering in unofficial French.

Thankfully, her office is toward the end of the passageway, a bit of a walk away from the main reception so, I assume she didn't hear much of it.

"I have no idea," I reply casually. "Why don't we get down to it?" I need to shake all thoughts of Theo out of my head.

I take a seat opposite her. "I know we usually have these one-to-ones online, but I wanted to discuss my leave as well, and I figured it's better to do it in person."

"Of course," she nods. She removes her glasses and sets them on the table. She claps her hands together, and now her full attention is on me.

"I also wanted to discuss what will happen to my job if I win the competition…" I speak slowly, not wanting to sound overconfident.

"Diana, you don't have to worry about your job. Yes, you must take unpaid leave, but you're a valued member of our team. And, if you win, it will be great publicity for AT." She smiles.

Well, that went a lot simpler than I expected. "All right, that's great, that's what I'll do."

"How's it coming along? You must do a public reading, right? Have you chosen your piece yet?" She looks at me intently.

"Yes, of course." I have chosen a few pieces, in fact, and I'm working on all of them. I want to have a backup plan, although I know this goes against Alia's suggestion of focusing on one piece and making it perfect.

"Are you coming?" I ask hopefully.

"Of course! As I said, it will be great publicity for AT. And I can't resist a good celebration for the written word," she circles her arms around her dramatically.

"Thanks, Kate, I'll see you at AFL."

"Good luck!" She sings as I walk out of her office.

I make my back to the elevators, keeping my head down. I really want to avoid another public row with Theo. Something is definitely off with him. First, he tells me that he broke up with Hilary, is happy to take things slow with me, then a few hours later decides to get back with her. And now he's upset that I didn't tell him about the competition.

And they say women are difficult to deal with.

Breathing a sigh of relief that I make it to the elevator without bumping into him, I hurry in and pushed the G button. Just as the doors close a familiar hand and watch, followed by a familiar shoulder pushes its way in.

Theo stands against the railing, hands in his pockets on the other side of the elevator. His eyes are moving up and down, studying me. I keep my gaze away, not wanting to initiate any conversation, although I'm glad I've made an extra effort today. I usually dress a lot more casually. However, today I'm wearing a black, wrap-around dress that comes to my shins and closed heels. My hair is pulled back in a sleek ponytail and I dabbed my face with concealer here and there to even out my skin tone. My lips are stained slightly with red lipstick. OK, I knew Theo would be here. I had to let him know what he was missing, even if his girlfriend could run for Miss Universe.

"I'm sorry about earlier," he says, breaking the silence with his deep voice. He took a step closer to me.

"I'm sorry I didn't tell you about the competition, I just didn't have the courage to speak to you again after you sent that text. Anyway, I hope you're happy." I say, trying to keep my voice even. The thought of him and Hilary together makes me want to cry and vomit at the same time.

"I didn't send you that text, Diana," he says calmly. He takes a step closer to me.

"I don't understand," I say, my mind scrambling around what he just said and the fact that he's coming closer to me and I can smell his cologne, making my legs turn to jelly.

"Hilary…she came over that night…she said she wanted to leave things on good terms. She must have sent the text while I was away or something and deleted the chat. I had no idea that you received that text. I thought you were shutting me out…"

"So, you're not disgusted by my allergy?"

He takes a step closer to me, trying to meet my gaze. "Do you really think I'm such a bastard?"

I shake my head, begging the tears to sink back to where they came from. "I don't know what to think, Theo. It wouldn't be the first time."

The elevator dings, and he moves to the side slightly, pushing the emergency stop button, and returns, moving closer to me. "I care about the excitement in your voice when you speak about the things you love." He grazes his thumb over my cheeks. I feel the warmth rising to my face.

"About the way your eyes sparkle when you're around your family." He brushes a single strand of hair away from my eyes.

"And I'm crazy about the way your hair falls to your shoulder, teasing me, begging me to place my lips on your sexy neck." His lips break into a soft curve.

"I'm known for my sexy neck." The words catch in my throat.

He holds the side of my face, brushing my cheek with his thumb. I take in his stormy eyes, his sharp nose, his strong jaw, and his alluring lips, calling my name, figuratively.

He presses his lips on to mine. My body melts as he takes me in his arms and the world dissolves around us. I inhale his spicy scent as if it's the only thing my lungs will accept. I don't need oxygen. I just need him.

What competition, what evil ex-girlfriend? It's me and Theo as one. And my heart, making it known that it's working very efficiently.

"Hello? Hello? Is anyone there? Is everything OK?" A voice crackles over the speaker.

We break away, I straighten my dress and Theo runs his hand through his hair. I bite my lip. Damn, I want him right now, on this floor. Wait, no, not the floor. Against the wall. Yes. No. Control yourself. I take a deep breath and gather my filthy thoughts.

"Hello, yes… everything is fine, I think I may have pushed the button by mistake," Theo replies apologetically.

"OK, no problem, I will open it for you, sir."

"Thank you," Theo grimaces.

The elevator dings open and we both walk out, looking slightly dishevelled. He stands with me while I wait for my Uber.

"What are we going to do?"

"I haven't figured that out yet, but we can't keep going like this." I jerk my head at what had just happened in the elevator. "We are going to get caught."

"Do you still want to take things slow? I miss you." He says impatiently, running his fingers through his hair again.

"I know I may be asking for a lot, Theo, but I think I need to settle things with Hilary first before we can move forward. I'm sorry."

The lines on Theo's forehead crease, "I understand; we have time."

A black Lexus arrives at the curb. Theo opens the door for me. "So, are we just not going to see each other?"

"For now, that's how it has to be. Bye, Theo," I peck him on the cheek and climb into the car.

Chapter 26

I lock the door of my apartment and drop the key into the bag hanging from my shoulder. As I begin pulling my suitcase toward the elevators, I hear Lucas's voice behind me.

"Diana."

Hearing his voice, my stomach sinks to my knees. I turn around slowly, wondering if he's holding a pickaxe. People deal with break-ups in different ways. Some take an extra yoga class. Some kill their ex. Why do I always associate this guy with murder?

"Lucas." My chest drops in relief seeing his hands in his pockets.

"I just wanted to wish you good luck, for your competition."

"Oh, thanks Lucas, it means a lot." I smile.

"See you around," he says. He waves and then enters his apartment.

"See ya."

That's kind of him. To remember that I was leaving for my competition today. I don't remember telling him much about it. I probably mentioned it at some point.

★★★★★★★★★★★★★

Rosie gives James a list of instructions followed by emergency numbers followed by instructions on how to reheat milk properly. She smothers her daughter with kisses and each time she takes a step forward to the car she runs back to give her baby another kiss.

She wipes away a tear. "Tears of joy," she jokes.

She climbs into the passenger seat and pulls on her seatbelt. I'm borrowing my parents' car. They'll be coming with Sam later in the evening.

We drive on the highway toward Dubai, most of it developed but a tedious drive, nonetheless. We reach our hotel after ninety minutes on the road, which doesn't feel like much because I have Rosie to keep me company. I update her on everything that happened with Theo.

She gives me advice on parenting (I tell her that she should save it for when I have a real relationship with someone who isn't a man-child or isn't the ex of my enemy). She describes the many ways she would like to 'inflict some pain' on 'Hilary fucking Dupont.' She also offers advice on dealing with Hilary if I see her at the festival doing the tour, quoting *The Art of War*.

"The art of war teaches us to rely not on the likelihood of the enemy not coming, but on our readiness to receive him," she says, reading from memory.

"Are we at war?" I squint quickly at Rosie before keeping my eyes on the road again.

"Of course, we are, this is Hilary Dupont we're talking about here. She's coming for you. I don't know if you stand a chance." Rosie replies with a goofy grin spreading across her face.

"Why don't you tell me what's really on your mind, hmm?" I say, grinning. I shake my head.

We drive into the reception parking of the Hilton in Jumeirah Beach Residence. We are immediately greeted by the valet. In a swish, our bags are unloaded, and our car is taken to be parked underground. Once we're inside, we check in and make our way to the rooms.

We're staying in Dubai for a day before the festival starts, to settle in before spending three full days at the festival. While some people commute every day to Dubai for work, I avoid the drive like the plague, until necessary. However, whenever I arrive in Dubai, I just soak in everything it has to offer and the memories of those tedious ninety minutes soon fade.

The large L-shaped bay windows ensure that every corner of the room is lit with sunlight. The room overlooks the splendid blue ocean. It's calm and the slight breeze ripples the water. The ocean is spotted with people swimming, soaking up the midday sun. It'll quieten toward the end of the day when the breeze leaves everyone feeling cold. Children are playing in the sand; ladies bathing on sun beds.

Envious of the midday sun that I hardly ever get to take advantage of, I turn my attention to Ain Dubai standing tall and proud on Bluewaters Island. I admire the wheel, and appreciate the enormity of it, remembering my splendid visit.

Rosie shuffles about behind me and then calls James. I don't pay any attention to the conversation, because firstly that would be eavesdropping and secondly, I have my shitty love life to fill my head instead.

What am I going to do about Hilary? Does she know that we know that she sent that text? Will Theo confront her? Did he do it already? Do I need to try and apologise to her again, this time in person so she has no option but to reply? Will she stop trying to sabotage my life if I do that? Aargh.

I close my eyes, in an effort to fight back the tears burning around them. That's another annoying thing. Every time I think about Theo, my throat gets blocked up; my chest becomes heavy and my eyes burn. Guilt consumes me too. Damn, it's more painful than being in the sun.

Rosie ends her call with a lot of kisses and finishes unpacking. I remain at the window, trying to pull myself together before putting on my happy relaxed face. I can speak to Rosie about these things. She'll listen. But this is her break for her too, and I can't burden her with my mess right now.

Once I unpack my essentials, we head downstairs. Thankfully, most of the direct sunlight is not on the beach so we decide to take a walk there before dinner, which is still an hour away.

We remove our flip-flops. Our feet sink into the cool sand, and we trudge all the way to the shore. As soon as we get to the wet sand, the cold water crashes onto our feet, making us both squeal. The air is cooling quickly; I regret not bringing a shawl to cover my shoulders.

Rosie stays on the side of the water, wetting her feet. I walk next to her trying to avoid the water, leaving footprints on the wet sand behind me. Most of the people have cleared out and the only ones apart from Rosie and I, are a couple who seems to be getting hot and heavy on their shared sun bed. Tourists, I'm sure, are probably not aware of the PDA rules in the Middle East. Rosie and I glance at each other than dart in the opposite direction.

She tells me about Sonia, and how much James helps her out. She tells me about all the new milestones Sonia has achieved. She's learning to sit; she smiles when people play with her; and she has a knack for blow-outs. I have no idea what that means but if I assume correctly, I'd rather not hear about it.

"Diana, I'm sorry I haven't been much support," she says.

"Rosie, you are no longer my editor. And Alia is great."

"I'm not talking about editing. I mean, with, you know, Theo and Lucas."

"You were there. You are always there every time I need to rant, and you are always there to listen. And it didn't work out either way. What happen with them was all my fault…I made poor decisions because I was desperate to not feel alone." I admit.

I empty the air from my lungs. "Rosie, we are here to win a competition. Not mull over boys. And I'm hungry." My tummy grumbles in agreement. I check my phone. 6.05. The buffet opened five minutes ago and I want to avoid the queues.

Rosie pulls me into a warm hug. "Let's go."

The restaurant is quiet. Chefs in their jackets and hats all stand diligently at their designated stations. The smell of food fills the air. People, mostly families with young children, trickle in and are seated by the waiting staff.

Following the rules for eating at a buffet, which come naturally to Rosie and me, we first scan everything on offer. Different types of sushi, a live pasta station, roasts, and prepared-to-order grilling stations. There's a salad bar with mixed salads and salad vegetables heaped in wooden bowls. Different types of dips and dressings. Pasta bakes, rice dishes, veggies, and curries fill silver chafing dishes. A bread station is piled high with rolls and freshly-baked loaves; Arabic bread slices are arranged in a basket beside sliced focaccia, and heaps of dinner rolls.

The dessert station is the highlight of my evening. At one end, various pots of gelato, ice creams, and sorbets are on display. In the front, there are rows of neatly-sliced tarts and layered cakes; on the left, there's a chocolate fountain, surrounded by skewered fruits and marshmallows. A steaming pot of *umm Ali* is on offer as well.

The memory of the buffet at the desert, where I'd explained the unsaid rules of buffet-eating to Theo, creeps into my mind. I miss him. My heart aches when I think about him. It feels like it all happened so long ago with another less vulnerable version of myself. I push him out of my mind as I sit down to eat.

I catch a glimpse of a familiar ponytail. I bolt up straight and panic shoots through me for a mere second. My eyes dart around the room.

"Is everything OK?" asks Rosie.

"I thought I saw Hilary." I scan every face I can see in the room before slumping back down. "I guess I was imagining it." I continue eating.

"She's given you PTSD."

"Not at all. It was just a trick of the light, I'm sure."

I smile at Rosie as I swirl a mound of spaghetti lathered generously with arrabbiata sauce, and shovel it into my mouth. My eyes can't help but steal a glance around every now and then when Rosie isn't looking just to make sure it was indeed just a trick of the light.

Chapter 27

The next day, bellies brimming with the most delightful breakfast offerings, we slowly make our way back to our room. We go over our itinerary for the day. I'll work on my chosen pieces. I don't even have to come clean to Rosie about choosing more than one piece. She didn't expect less, she let me know with an exasperated sigh.

As soon as the sun comes down a notch, around five p.m., we'll take a taxi to Dubai Media City. Thankfully the festival runs on Saturday, Sunday, and Monday from ten o'clock in the morning to ten o'clock in the evening. If I miss certain authors during the day, it was possible to catch them on the next day, most probably at night.

The taxi drops us off at the entrance. The sun is already turning from golden yellow to orange, which means I'm safe outside, but I still apply sun cream all over me, just in case. The evening is cool, and having learned from the night before, I wear a thin jumper over my dress.

Barricades line the place, cordoning off entrance and exit points. There are queues at the entrance but, thankfully, there's a separate queue for VIP passes. We go through swiftly, and a lady in a security guard uniform checks our bags. We take a map from the kiosk stand to work out where we're going.

The sky is darkening but the entire area is brightly lit. We pass the kids' area, where children's authors are holding workshops and readings. It's all done up in playful colours and beanbags. We pass a number of food trucks. All of them have long queues. Let's face it: people will go to any festival, just for the food. So much for the cardinal rule of book care: don't eat while handling a book. Clearly not cardinal any more.

There are a few workshops and panel discussions going on in some tents. Judging by the signs, the tents, the workshops or panel discussions are either about Emirati and Arabic poetry by local talent, or topics based on shaping young minds for the future and the future of literature.

This year, one of my favourite authors, Maggie Claire, is holding a reading at the festival. Rosie has me taking actual notes of how she presents herself. After the reading, I seize one of Maggie Clare's books from the shelf and join the queue of excited fellow-readers to have it signed. Next, we go to the tent where they have books on sale. People are buzzing around tables, sifting through enormous piles of books. Rosie and I part ways and agree to meet back at the entrance. Both holding more books than our hands can carry, we meet at the entrance and make our way back.

At the hotel room, we offload all our books onto the little side tables, kick the shoes off our aching feet, and collapse into the cloud-like hotel beds.

I toss and turn all night. The small lights from the TV or the fire alarm disturb the peace I usually find in the dark. Rosie snores softly into her pillow. I'm pretty sure this is the best sleep she's had since she became pregnant.

I keep going over my chosen reading piece in my head. I can't help wondering if I've made the right choice, or if I should have chosen another. Every time I drift off to sleep, either a shuffling noise or a voice from outside wakes me up. Defeated, I rise from the bed. I gather my hair and splash cold water onto my face. I should go for a run. The fresh air will help clear my mind. But I don't make it out of our suite. Once my eyes fully adjust to the dark, I pace the living room, in the hope that I don't disturb Rosie's deep slumber.

Positive thoughts, positive thoughts, positive thoughts.

****

After Rosie wakes up, we make our way down for breakfast. I sip water and terribly bitter coffee. My stomach is in knots. But I need the caffeine if I'm to survive the day.

The dining area is crawling with people. I study the reading program. There it is, printed on the program. Diana Dawson. My name is under the heading that says 'Contestants.' I'll be on at two p.m. I bite my lip. I make a mental note to take my antihistamines as soon as I get back upstairs. I really hope we'll be in a tent doing readings, as opposed to out in the direct sun.

I see the familiar swish of the ponytail again. This time it isn't my imagination. The evil being of Hilary Dupont is towering over me. Her hair is pulled up in her regular high tail, her perfect body showing through her perfectly tailored navy jumpsuit. There's a diamond bracelet on her wrist, and stones to match on her ears. I take in her perfection with disgust and envy. Her eyes are bright, and her grin stretches from one diamond-encrusted ear to the other. She only smiles this way when she has a plan cooked up to sabotage someone. Usually that someone is me.

"Diana Dawson. Hope you're enjoying breakfast." She tips her head to my untouched plate of bits and pieces.

"I suddenly lost my appetite." I retort, keeping my expression neutral.

Maybe she expects me to sympathise with myself. Her face straightens up. "You won't have that attitude for long, babe. You'll wish you'd never met me."

"Do whatever you want. I don't care." I say, rolling my eyes. Obviously, I do care, so very, very much. My insides are cringing. But should I let my enemy know that she's truly getting to me? No. I can't let her think she's winning. Is that a rule in the *Art of War*? I should ask Rosie.

She puts her hands down on my table and shoves her face in front of mine, I can see that her pores are non-existent and now I feel more conscious that she can see my very existent pores which makes me kind of freak out more than the fact of her trying to ruin my career. Wow, Diana, you've got your priorities straight.

People are craning their necks to get a glimpse of the impromptu morning entertainment.

Now the blood starts to bubble inside me. I stand up so quickly, she almost stumbles back. Even Rosie gapes at me. "Get a life, Hilary. Stop obsessing over mine."

"My *life* was ruined when you told everyone about my parents," she seethes. "Nice little stunt I must admit."

"It wasn't a stunt Hilary, and *I* didn't *tell* anyone about your parents, and you know it. And I apologised." I look around the hall at the gaping faces. "Rosie let's go." Rosie slumps in the chair, her mouth pouting, full of the breakfast offerings. I widen my eyes and she quickly gulps and shovels a bit more food in, before leaving with me.

"I'm not done with you, Diana Dawson," Hilary threatens as we walk away.

I turn around, shooting her a fake grin. "Looking forward to it."

****

I pull up my washed-out high-waisted denim and roll up the sleeves of my white shirt. I drag the brush through my hair and straighten its ends with a hair iron. I reach into my bag searching for my antihistamines. Hand cream, hand sanitizer, spare masks, sunglasses, wallet, lip balm. No antihistamines.

I empty out my bag on the bed and go through each item again. I swear I packed them in here. I rummage through my suitcase. I empty out all my clothing, pushing my hands through every pocket in the suitcase. Nothing.

Rosie steps out of the bathroom. She gasps. "What's going on?"

A lump begins forming in my throat. My armpits began to sweat. My breathing is now rapid. I've forgotten the most important thing.

"Diana, are you all right?"

Tears stream down my face as I come to a realisation of how the rest of this day is going to go.

"I've forgotten my medication." It's hard to believe that these words are coming out of my mouth. It's like watching a bad movie in slow motion. I'm pretty sure that I had packed it. I know I scratched it off the list.

Rosie dresses quickly and comes to hold me. "We are going to figure this out," she says reassuringly.

I finally stop sobbing and clean up my face. I apply sun cream twice. Hopefully, it'll be enough to get through the reading. I read the piece to Rosie one more time, trying to forget that there'll be a very good chance that my performance will turn into a really bad break-dance instead. And they'll disqualify me just for that. I bet Hilary will have a good laugh to know I've somehow sabotaged myself.

Trying to rid my head of all my worst nightmares, as they seem to have manifested right before my eyes, Rosie pulls me out of the room.

We arrive at the festival at one o'clock. The reading is starting in half an hour. According to the program, I'm after Samantha Brown and a piece from *Into The Red*, her latest novel. It's fiction for sure. Sounds psychological. Wondering about her book distracts me from my current mess. I wonder what she thinks when she sees the title of my book 'The Monster Inside Me: The Other Side of the Forest.' I'm certainly intrigued. And I'd written the book. And I may be biased.

My eyes rest on our stage. Which is in direct sunlight. Of course. I can hear mumbled complaints about it, although some audience members love being outside, finally soaking in some of the vitamin D that the summer months have deprived them of.

I stand near a neighbouring reading, which is under a tent, for as long as I can. There is a good turn-out in front of our stage. On the right of the podium, the judges are seated about a meter away; chatting to each other, shuffling forms around, scribbling notes. I catch a glimpse of Hilary, sitting with the other judges, fiddling with a pen in her hand. At the end of Samantha's reading, the audience clapped.

Rosie and Alia walk toward me. "Look who I found," Rosie says.

"Alia, I am so glad you could make it. I thought you weren't coming." I hug her, I really hope I make her proud.

"I wasn't going to, I had a family thing, but I couldn't sit there wondering how your reading was going," she pauses. "I sent you a message."

"You did? Oh." I pull out my phone to check for new messages.

She does the same. "Oh dear, I typed the message, didn't hit 'Send.' I'm so sorry,"

"It happens to the best of us, and you're here anyway. Why don't you guys grab a seat? I'll be up there in a few."

"Good luck." they both squeal, making their way to the seats in the first row. I keep an eye out for my parents who arrive promptly at one fifty-five p.m. They give me a quizzical look. I point up to the tent, and they both nod in understanding.

I wonder once more whose bright idea it had been to have the reading out in the open. Everyone is wearing sunglasses. Except me. I can't because I'm doing the reading. I make a mental note to complain to whoever is in charge.

I make my way toward the stage. I step onto it and scan the audience.

I take a deep breath to calm the butterflies in my stomach, the nerves swirling around my mind, registering the tiny ants who've already come out to play. I flip the pages of my book to the chapter I'm reading.

I smile at my parents in the crowd; their faces are gleaming with pride. Rosie and Alia are seated in the front row. Hilary is sitting quite upright with her chin up. More ants crawl all over my body.

I spot a familiar face in the crowd. It's Theo. He's come to see me read. I try not to focus on him, but our eyes meet more than a few times. His lips curve into a slight smile, and my heart does the little hop it's become accustomed to doing whenever I see him, think about him, or hear his voice. Kate is seated next to him, wearing sunglasses too large for her face. I can spot her red nails all the way from the stage.

I open my mouth, but no voice comes out. My throat is as dry as the desert I live in. My legs feel as if they're made from water. Itching all over! I've had enough. This is it. I don't want to feel sorry for myself. I don't want to keep panicking every time I don't take any medication or apply enough sunblock.

"Good afternoon, ladies and gentlemen. Firstly, I would like to thank all of you for coming out here today. I am really excited to be here. Before I start my reading, I have a confession to make. But this goes against all the coaching I've had from my editor for my public reading, I'm sorry, Alia." I tip my head humbly in her direction.

The crowd murmurs laughter.

"Right now, as I stand in this delightful sun, my body is itching, all over. And, I am probably going to turn into a nasty shade of red very soon… because I am allergic to the sun."

People look at each other unsure of what's happening. But to me, it feels as if I have lifted a weight off my chest. A weight that had been there for twenty years. The weight of the sun.

"I would normally apologise to you if you saw me this way…but this is who I am, and I've decided that I'm no longer going to be ashamed of something that is beyond my control." I glance at my parents. Dad wipes his eye with the back of his hand.

"Also, I may break out into a weird squirm slash jig when I get really itchy, and you're welcome to join in." The crowd laughs and I pick up a few nervous glances my way.

"Now, onto what Jamie and Isabella are getting up to."

I read my passage. My legs no longer feel like water and my voice is smooth and firm and eloquent.

My reading had been engaging and entertaining after all. My body is burning now. I thank the audience and hurry off the stage.

Mum jogs over to me, quickly pulling a bottle of antihistamines out of her bag. She hands it to me and then pulls me in for a tight squeeze.

"That was beautiful sweetheart. I am so proud of you," she smiles warmly. "And I can't wait to read your latest book," she murmurs affectionately. Dad, Rosie, Sam, Kate, and Alia come over as well. Whatever the outcome, I did what I had to do, and it was over.

Chapter 28

He is leaning on an information board, with a sly smirk spreading across his handsome face. I head toward him, touched and surprised that he has come to my reading. As I walk closer to him, I notice him shaking a familiar white bottle in his hand.

"Looking for something?" he asks, as I near him.

I peer at the bottle closely. It's my medication.

"You took my medication," I say, feeling surprisingly calm.

Lucas laughs.

"Why would you do that?"

"Oh, I loved watching you squirm up there on that stage."

"What is wrong with you, Lucas?" I try to snatch the bottle out of his hands but he moves his hand away swiftly so that I miss.

"You know, Diana. Payback is a bitch." He cocks his head. "Like you." He smirks again.

"Are you still upset that I broke up with you?" I try to keep my voice steady, but the calm is overtaken by the urge to punch that stupid smirk off Lucas's face.

"Broke up with me? Oh, you didn't even have the decency to do that. You put it on a Post-it note," he spits.

"I apologised."

"Didn't your mummy ever tell you that 'sorry' is not enough?" he mocks.

This has just confirmed my belief that considering Lucas as a child was not an exaggeration, if ever I had any doubts before.

Before I realise what's happening, my knuckles connect to his jaw, sending shooting pain through my hand. His face barely moves, and my knuckles feel as if they've been shattered into tiny pieces. He rubs his jaw and laughs. Yes, quite immature I admit, but it was my body's natural response to plain ol' evil.

"Oooh, she's a wild one," I hear a voice say.

I turn around to see Hilary walking up to us. Now I'm surprised.

"All right there, darling? Did Diana find her pills?"

She laughs. Lucas pulls her in, and they kiss sloppily. Yurgh.

"So how did this happen?" I say, wagging my finger between the two of them, swallowing the bile rising in my throat.

"Theo, actually. When I came down to pay him a little visit, he couldn't stop talking about you and your boyfriend. He bored me to death with the details of why Lucas was not the right guy for you, and he couldn't figure out what you saw in him." She rolls her eyes. "Then I realised that the idiot has feelings for you. And you know what, I wasn't even surprised, you are always at the centre of everything that goes wrong in my life."

Dramatic much. I wouldn't say *everything*.

"And so, I decided to pay Lucas a little visit and imagine my surprise, or lack of it, when he told me that you broke up with him because you had feelings for your editor. You can say that we bonded over our broken hearts." She pouts her lips. "I just had to get on that panel, thanks to Daddy's many contacts in the business. And now, little Diana Dawson, the fate of your career lies in my hands." She beams with pride. "Lucas's charm got me a key to your room," she adds nonchalantly. She pecks him on the lips. "Thanks, babe."

"Wow, stealing my medication from my bag. How original." I smirk at Hilary. I try to compose myself as best as possible. I'm not going to let them think that they've got under my skin. Even though they really have.

I leave them praising themselves for their 'master plan' and meet my parents and Rosie, who are waiting for me. My hand still feels the effects of that punch. I smile to myself. I didn't know I had it in me.

"What was that all about?" Rosie asks quietly. "Who was that man with Hilary?"

"That's Lucas," I said quietly.

"Lucas?" She gasps. She hasn't met Lucas before. "Wow," she mouths.

"Yeah, I know."

"He is gorgeous!" She turns to gape at him again.

"Rosie!"

She turns back to me. "I'm sorry. It's not every day you see a man like that. Why did you break it off?"

I nudge her. "You're missing the point."

"Fine, fine, Lucas bad, Lucas bad," she chants, bringing her hands to her eyes and pushing them forward to show me she's focused.

"Yes, he is worse than I'd thought if Hilary got through to him. And to think I felt sorry for him…"

Rosie rubs my arm. "You're better off without him. And if he's with Hilary, he's obviously an idiot. So how did they end up together?"

"I'll fill you in later," I sigh. "But he is the one who took my antihistamines from my bag."

Chapter 29

I step out of the shower and wrap the warm, soft gown around my body. My skin no longer burns, but it does ache slightly. I'm looking forward to the soft luscious hotel bed that I didn't manage to enjoy the night before.

I hear voices as I leave the bathroom. Theo is standing in the 'lounge' with Rosie. They suddenly stop talking.

"I'm hungry again, I'm going to see what's left of the buffet," Rosie says casually and quickly leaves the room.

Theo has bags around his eyes, and his face is unshaven for what looks like a few days. My throat begins to close in slowly and my heart flutters. It's good to see him again. I owe him an explanation, though. Why I want things to be the way they are, for now, or at least why I wanted to be away from him. Seeing him standing there, studying me, waiting for me, every nerve in my body wants to be with him, in his arms. I finally speak, letting the truth come out unaltered.

"Theo…I'm sorry for pushing you away…I felt guilty for having feelings for you because you were Hilary's boyfriend."

"I'm not following. What does Hilary have to do with any of this?"

"It was in high school… and I apologised many times, but she hasn't forgiven me… and now… you and me having feelings for each other…has given her more reason to quench her thirst for revenge…"

I tell him the story of the note and the class idiot. "I feel guilty because I should have handled everything differently. I didn't need to give that note to her in front of other people. I could have kept the note to myself. I could have waited till she was alone to return the note. I feel guilty for exposing something that was private. I wish I had done things differently…I had forgotten about her until the day we met again…and the guilt just came flooding back."

"Diana," he gazes into my eyes and cups my face. "What happened between you two was a long time ago. And you apologised. Hilary needs to move on. And so should you."

He moves closer to me. He traces circles on the edge of my jaw with his thumb. "I want to touch you and hold you. I want to listen to everything you have to say. I just want to be wherever you are."

"That's not creepy at all," I smile.

He crushes his lips onto mine.

He slips off the gown from my shoulder and caresses my cheek. Moving wet hair from my face, he continues, "I don't care about AT; I don't care about Hilary's threats." He slips the gown off my other shoulder and left it to fall to the floor. "I want us to make this work, what we have right now."

Chapter 30

The crisp air smacks against my face, bringing balance to my body, which is increasing in warmth. My lungs burn; sweat rolls down my face; and my mind swirls with the events from the previous night as I run along the calm waters of Jumeirah Beach.

Rosie texted to say she was spending the night at my parents' suite. Theo was still in bed when I left. He slept soundly. Every kiss, every touch, every moment had brought us closer together.

I feel like a new person. A new, very-nervous-of-what-the-day-was-going-to-bring person.

When I get back, Theo is dressed. He doesn't join me for breakfast. We want to avoid any conversation with Rosie and my family about what had happened between us. So, he leaves and goes back to his own hotel. He'll meet me at the festival.

My stomach is still in knots, for various reasons, so I nibble on fruit. I don't need any coffee; every sound, every touch makes me feel jumpy. I'm still worried about Hilary's next plot for revenge. Her words 'The fate of your career is in my hands,' still ring in my ear. She's definitely very confident. Rosie thinks it's just a threat to throw me off. But I know better.

Once we arrive, we make our way through the entrance gates, once more and settle down in the seats near the stage. I let out a sigh of relief when I notice that we are under the tent today. Why didn't they do that yesterday when I was burning in the sun? No. Stop right there. The new Diana embraces her allergy.

"You're glowing," Rosie grins, wiggling her eyebrows. She locks her arm in mine as we walk to the seating area.

"I'm not," I insist, fighting to keep my face from smiling.

"Someone got laid last night," she sings, and then unlocks from my arm and pushes her hips back and forth.

"Rosie!" I grab her arms back to me and she hunches over in hysterical laughter. I need new friends.

I look around, hoping no one caught sight of us.

"I'm excited for you. Do you even remember how to do it? How long has it been?"

"Three years, five months, and fourteen days," I say, lifting my chin up. "Not that I'm counting." We both snort laughter.

"I should pass on my copy of the modern-day Karma Sutra."

"The what now?"

"Yes, I'm an expert now, it'll be like a master passing on the torch to her student. James and I have a great sex-life thanks to that book, and I'd be doing you a disservice if I didn't share the secrets to mind-blowing—"

"Please go on and flood my brain with more images of you and James in bed," I say deadpan.

Rosie's eyes light up for a second. "Really?" she bares her teeth. "You're my best friend, I will share *everything* with you—"

"No!" I practically scream. "I appreciate it," I say, steadying my voice. "But no."

Rosie's lips droop into a pout and she bats her eyelashes.

I shake my head and pull her in, pressing my face against her head. "You're a mad woman and I love you, Rosana Patel."

Rosie has made all the nerves disappear for a short moment.

✴✴✴✴✴✴✴✴✴✴✴✴✴✴✴

All the contestants are in the front row. My palms are sweaty; my heart thumps louder and louder in my chest. I hope the person next to me doesn't hear it. I tap my feet on the ground, drum my fingers on my knees, waiting for the judges to arrive. They take their seats at their table. If they moved any slower they'd be moving backward. Each judge announces the winners for each category in turn.

Now, it's time for them to call out the winner for the young adult fiction category. There we go. I squeeze my eyes shut, my ears on high alert for what they're about to say next.

"Diana Dawson, for 'The Monster Inside Me: The Other Side of the Forest,'" a voice calls out.

I take a moment to wonder if they have actually called my name and if I didn't imagine it. My stomach flips and my heart jumps, almost out through my mouth, wanting to run away and scream, with its tiny hands up in the air.

I step onto the stage and accept my award. My hand brushes over the frosted glass with the AFL slogan on it. On a shiny wooden block, my name is engraved. It is the most beautiful, most precious thing I own. Everything around me is a blur as I get down from the raised platform.

Rosie, Alia, and my parents run over to congratulate me pulling me for tight hugs and sloppy kisses on the cheek. Other people whom I've never met come to shake my hand. Sam pats me on the back because he's too cool for hugs, and he has a reputation to protect.

My cheeks hurt from the constant smiling and grinning. Relief, pride, and joy all wash over me at the same time.

Suddenly, we hear raised voices behind us. We all turn to see what the arguing is about. Up on stage, a rather dishevelled-looking Hilary is stamping her feet and growling at some of the other judges. It's not hard for me to flash a wide smile at her when she looks at me, narrowing her eyes, trying to pierce me with her daggers. I won after all, despite her best efforts.

I glance down again at my most prized possession, just to make sure it's still in my hand. I search the crowd for Theo; he's standing by himself leaning against the wall. His face shines with pride. As I near him, he hurries to me and pulls me into a hug, lifting me off my feet, and burying his face into my neck. I inhale his delicious scent. It brings a calmness over me, and for a moment I feel that everything around us has melted away. His embrace warms my chest and makes my heart glow even brighter.

A woman clears her throat behind us. Theo sets me down, as the heat rises to my cheeks.

"I'm sorry," I say, feeling very aware of her eyes on me.

"Congratulations on your win, Miss Dawson."

"Thank you," I say. Everything still feels a bit surreal.

She holds out a small white envelope. "This is all the information you will need to move on to the next process. A meeting with our managers will be set up for you, and they will be in touch."

I take the envelope from her. I turn it over in my hands, making sure that it is indeed real. I open it under her gaze, just to check that it has my name on it, and there it is. Diana Dawson. That is all I need to see. I slip the card back into the envelope.

"Congratulations again, Miss Dawson. All the best." With that, she walks off.

My phone vibrates. It's a text from Rosie. She's joined Mum and Dad at one of the food trucks, and then they'll be on their way home. I reply, telling her I'll join her soon.

Theo takes my hand, which fits perfectly in his.

He twirls me around, and I spin straight into his firm chest. He leans down to kiss me, but I cover his lips with my fingers.

"I'd rather not get arrested before my flight to New York."

Theo straightens his shoulders suddenly and his face loses all emotion. I turn around to see what he's looking at.

Hilary stomps over to us, eyelashes wet, make-up smudged, hair dishevelled. I have to admit I've never gloated more than to see her this way.

Theo takes a step forward, I put my arm out in front of him. I look up at him as he opens his mouth to object. "I need to do this OK?"

"I'm not yet done with you Diana Dawson," she growls. I roll my eyes. Here we go again. "I have friends in high places—"

"Stop, Hilary! Just stop!" I cry over her. I have had more than enough of her threats over the past few months. "Stop trying to sabotage me, stop threatening me, just stop! We are moving on with our lives; you need to, as well."

"You destroyed my parents'—"

"No, *I* didn't. Your parents' marriage was obviously already on the rocks." I won't say more, I don't want to risk embarrassing her further. "Stop blaming *me,* Hilary. Blame your parents, blame the media but not me! Yes, I found that letter, yes, I should have handled that note better but those were the honest mistakes of an eighteen-year-old. I could have easily used it after you got me kicked off the committee, but my intention was to return it to you, discreetly."

She just watches me, lips pouted, nose slightly wet.

"Bye, Hilary, have a nice life." I spin around, taking Theo by the arm, and walk away, happy that I've finally confronted her and made peace with myself, too.

We meet my parents, Sam and Rosie at the food truck. We gobble down warm shawarmas and sip on icy soda while we chat about the festival, the food, and our trip back home.

"So, when do *we* leave for New York?" Theo asks, before putting a French fry between his lips.

My heart and face beam at his question. I realise we've never spoken about what will happen if I did win. Why hadn't we?

"You're coming with me to New York?"

He takes my hand and brings it to his lips. He kisses it gently, sending electricity shooting throughout my body. "When I said that I wanted to be with you wherever you are, I meant it."

I smile and lean over, closer to him, I can see the creases around his silver eyes, and I can smell his decadent scent which causes me to replay images of last night in my head. "Still creepy."

He grins and moves away, sipping his soda. "I can't wait to show you, New York."

He's coming with me. I wouldn't have to figure out how to make a long-distance relationship work. I wouldn't have to stay awake to video-call him at an unreasonable time, we wouldn't have to align our schedules to spend holidays together. Yes, obviously those thoughts have crossed my mind. Obviously, I've thought about whether to ask him to move in with me, because, no offense to Al Reem Island, but Saadiyat Island has a beach.

Not only do I have an incredibly supportive partner to tread this new path with me, but I came out, literally too—about my sun allergy. It no longer causes me shame. I'm longer afraid to stand at the top of Burj Khalifa and scream out to the world: "I'm allergic to the sun, and I'm proud of the woman I've become!" Hopefully, there won't be a need for that because, you know, the tallest building in the world, and falling to your death and everything.

I look around the table at my family, chatting, enjoying their meals, and patting on the back (again). We've all come a long way. This achievement is not only mine. It's theirs too. They've been cheering me on from the word go.

There's just one more thing left to do. Get on that 'New York Times Bestsellers' list!

THE END